The man was still perhaps twenty feet away, but making toward her with a set of his features unusual for a tourist. She reached out instinctively for Eric, but the little boy was several feet away. Margaret took a step forward, but the man was there first, brushing between them.

She put a hand up to her throat to scream, but his hand got there first and clamped down over her mouth.

"I told you, lady, to stop messing around in other people's business, but you wouldn't listen—"

Margaret managed to utter a short sentence before his crushing hand squeezed her lips closed.

"Don't hurt the boy."

"Oh no, the boy has a long future ahead of him. I'm sorry I can't say the same for you. . . ."

Also by Richard Barth:

DEADLY CLIMATE*
THE CONDO KILL
ONE DOLLAR DEATH
THE RAG BAG CLAN*
A RAGGED PLOT**

**Published by Fawcett Books*

***Forthcoming from Fawcett Books*

BLOOD DOESN'T TELL

Richard Barth

FAWCETT CREST • NEW YORK

A Fawcett Crest Book
Published by Ballantine Books

Library of Congress Catalog Card Number: 88-29872

ISBN 0-449-21797-3

This edition published by arrangement with St. Martin's Press, Inc.

Manufactured in the United States of America

First Ballantine Books Edition: May 1990

This is for Jenny, wherever she may be.

One

TEN FEET AWAY FROM THE DOUBLE DOORS she stopped her cart and hit the wall switch. It was at elbow height and positioned in such a way that the nurses and doctors never had to break stride from one of their rolling stretchers. The ten-foot interval was just enough to allow the electric doors to open before the bed glided through the opening. In Margaret's case, her cartload of books didn't need to be rushed through to surgery or X ray or CAT scan or the half dozen other destinations in the hospital complex, so she waited until the doors were fully open, then pushed against the cart again.

Thursdays at Metropolitan Hospital were one of the high points of her week. There were a hundred ways she could spend her free mornings and afternoons, but none was as important or even as interesting as her work with the volunteer library book cart. On days when her arthritis wasn't acting up, she'd double stack the top shelf to wind up with a selection of over eighty books. The backs of her legs would feel it that night, but the stiffness was nothing that a good hot bath wouldn't cure.

Her customers, in a hospital the size of Metropolitan, one of New York's large public institutions, numbered in the many hundreds. Anyone who could hold their head high enough to watch "The Cosby Show" could look at what she had to offer. And any day she came back after her three-hour tour with more than ten or fifteen books left on the top shelf was a day she considered less than successful.

Of course she had some easy sales. Old Mrs. Rosenwasser in the cardiac care unit read a mystery a day, preferably one of the English cosies like Christie or Sayers. Then there was Mr. Hemphill over in the psychiatric section who had to have a history book every week, preferably dealing with the Napoleonic wars, though in a pinch he'd settle for the broader category of Western Europe up to and including the treaty of Vereeniging. Margaret had a list of about ten patients whom she shopped for in the hospital's library every week, but it was the transients who gave her all the headaches. If she loaded up on sports books and police procedurals, then wouldn't you know it they'd ask for fashion and home decorating books. If she slipped into the obstetrics ward stocked up with sewing and knitting manuals, what would they want—books on stock-market analysis or personality development, of all things. She could never outguess them although she had tried every Thursday for the last three years.

But her joy did not really come from emptying her cart. That was incidental. If Margaret Binton had excelled in anything in her seventy-two years it was in the art of conversing. She was nothing less than a black-belt kibitzer and proud of it. She wouldn't just place the book she'd found on the seige of Mafeking on Hemphill's bed and walk away. The delivery would probably take over twenty minutes and in that time they might touch on such diverse topics as Bill Bradley's chances for 1992, the best way to remove cigarette burns from light wooden furniture, how to fake a pesto sauce without pignoli nuts, or maybe the weather in Florida where Margaret had just come from on vacation. At least that's what they talked about last time, when Margaret had brought *The Diplomatic History of the American People, 1802 to 1865* and plopped it down on his bed. But today she really wanted to talk about the Darryl Strawberry deal, which meant Peter Ryker up on ten . . . she knew he was still around. Hemphill hadn't the least interest in the Mets. She pushed the cart down the corridor toward the elevators and the osteopathic ward.

Ryker spotted her five minutes later the moment she arrived on the tenth-floor ward, his home for the past three and a half weeks. It was past eleven o'clock, so he had already gotten over his wake-up depression and was actually in a good mood. The sight of the trim little old lady with gray hair pushing the book cart up the aisle brought probably the only smile of the day to his face. He waited patiently as she negotiated with the several other patients closer to the doorway, wondering what it was that made her different from the other six volunteers. Her age, for one thing. Most of the others were younger and looked like they were doing this gig to assuage their guilt at having to lunch at some swank Madison Avenue restaurant and then shop for the rest of the afternoon at Bendel's. He didn't mind that. Hell, he liked looking at expensive faces. But Margaret had a resoluteness and definition to her that the doctors' and lawyers' wives couldn't approach. She had an intelligent, old-world sense of humor, not brassy or forced, and could be counted on to deliver a solid twenty minutes of entertainment every Thursday. He looked angrily up at his leg in traction as he felt a little rivulet of pain shoot across the back of his knee. Ligaments growing back—or maybe it was the bone reknitting. Whatever . . . it would take a few more weeks before they dropped the leg and he could get off his back. He shifted his other leg and slid his torso an inch to the left. The pain went away slightly, but not enough to suit him. What a goddamn awful position, he thought. One of the best cityside reporters for *Newsday* flat on his ass for a month . . . and why . . . for some silly ski weekend in March when the snow was like mashed potatoes anyway. His Staten Island corruption story had to be handed off to Wilberts, known affectionately in the city room as "Old Schooner" for his affinity toward liquid lunches. Serves me right, Ryker thought, March is for the NCAAs anyway.

"So," she interrupted his thoughts. "Think they should have given Strawberry the ten million?"

Ryker turned his head away from his bandaged leg and focused on her. He'd interviewed enough people in his ten years at the paper to pride himself on his ability to see evidence of their character in their faces. Margaret's was as open as a portrait by Foujita . . . perhaps not quite as innocent. The wrinkles at the corners of her eyes only served to widen their good-humored sparkle. Her nose was peasantlike, solid and honest. She made no compromises or apologies to age; gray was gray, which was the color of her hair, pulled back neatly in a tight little bun at the back of her head. It was an old lady's face, but one of quiet strength. Ryker had only seen it smiling.

"They're crazy," he answered. "Ten million for a guy like Strawberry . . . 's peanuts." He shook his head and tried to scooch a little higher in bed. Margaret fluffed his pillow after he resettled. "He puts more fannies in the seats than anyone in New York, he and Gooden. Hell, I'd give him twenty million if he asked for it."

"Ten million for four years . . ." Margaret thought out loud. "That's enough to feed all the homeless people on the streets of New York for the rest of their lives."

Ryker chortled. "Homeless people don't hit forty home runs a season and have over one hundred RBIs." He leaned closer to her cart and tried to catch some of the titles. "You got anything worth reading?"

"What a cynic," she said. "You must be feeling good today. Janet come by before work?"

He pulled a book out halfway, looked at its cover, then pushed it back. "Yeah, but you know how wives are. No sympathy. She thinks this is a vacation for me . . . as if I enjoy being trussed up like a Georgia pig before a family reunion." Margaret looked at the remaining books and after a moment, pulled one out. "*Ball Four*," she said. "Bouton's book. You'll love it."

"Already read it."

"Oh." She rummaged some more. "Here. One on the 'fifty-eight Packers."

"Not in the mood. Football season's over." He reached out and pulled a tall volume onto his lap, *Flora and Fauna of the Southwest Kalahari Desert*. He looked up at her with a grin. "People actually ask for these things?"

"Hey," she said. "Broaden your mind. Impress your fellow reporters. How many other people you know can describe a yellow-tailed Barnett's dickey?"

He flipped through a few pages and handed it back. "Margaret, I don't exactly see giving Mr. Barnett's namesake houseroom in my overcluttered brain cells, cute and just as yellow as he may be. How about a good thriller? MacInnes or Ambler."

"You're better than that," Margaret said and pulled out another volume. "Here, Toni Morrison, and I'm not taking it back.'' She pushed the cart a foot further away and sat down on his bed. ''So how's the leg feeling?''

''About the same. I should have remembered that skiing's a white man's sport.''

''Oh come on,'' Margaret said. She looked at his grinning face, the color of sanded teak, and laughed. ''I suppose you fell because of some honky trailgroomer . . . or maybe the snow blinded you because it was too white?''

''Enough, enough, you're right. You don't have to be black to go careening out of control into a tree.'' He picked up the book and put it on his night table. ''Thanks. I never read Morrison.''

''About a few weeks more?'' Margaret asked and patted his hand.

He nodded. ''While Wilberts messes up the story. By the time I get out it'll be as cold as last year's batting averages.''

''Hey,'' Margaret said getting up. ''There'll always be another story. Good reporters like you always find them.''

''Thanks,'' he said and grimaced as the pain shot back through his knee joint. ''If I'm not out of here soon I think I'll do one on hospital cruelty. After all, goddamn it, I've done all the research.''

She took a break after finishing the obstetrics section. Not a bad day so far, only seven new books left (she had collected some returns on the bottom shelf) and still over twenty minutes before she was expected back with the cart. She was sitting in the waiting room with all the expectant relatives, her favorite waiting room in the entire hospital. No one got down on her for lighting up one of her morning cigarettes . . . no one even noticed. Once she had tried it in the cardiac waiting room and four people screamed at her. Also, cadging was a cinch. There were enough smokers to go around for a company of GIs on a five-minute break. Margaret inhaled deeply, crushed the Camel out in an ashtray, and stood up to head back. She was thinking of how she was going to spend the rest of the day when she absently turned left on the fifth-floor corridor leading into the Frudenthal wing, rather than right down towards the C bank of elevators. When she realized her mistake she had already made several more turns and was hopelessly lost. There were a lot of private laboratories and medical offices and very few patients. She kept walking in the blind faith that corridors usually end in elevator banks.

But this particular corridor ended in a set of closed doors. Margaret was pushing against the right-hand one when a nurse emerged from the other one.

"Can I help you?" the nurse said with a quizzical expression on her face. She was looking down into Margaret's book cart.

"Yes," Margaret answered politely. "I'm trying to find my way down to the library on the first floor."

"Second left turn," The nurse said icily and pointed in the direction Margaret had just come. "Ain't no one inside here can read a book." She marched off and turned into one of the nearby offices. Margaret stood still for a moment thinking about the peculiar answer. Where had she gotten to, the morgue? No, she remembered, that was down in the basement. Some ophthalmologic unit where people had bandaged eyes? A burn ward? Maybe she could find some Braille books in the library. Cautiously she pushed at the door again, leaving her cart behind. The doors opened into a short corridor with six rooms fanning off, three on a side. It was a small area about the size of her apartment, lit brightly with fluorescent lights and smelling slightly off-key, something like the bathroom downstairs at Stark's coffee shop on 89th Street. But what immediately brought her up short was the noise, the sound of at least a dozen tiny voices—babies crying. The sound was not loud, not like they were in pain really. And whimpering didn't place it either. More like a steady resigned whining, something they produced as naturally as the effluent from their bodies. Margaret frowned and stuck her head around one of the doorways, bracing herself for the shock of the expected maimed, burned, or diseased child. What she saw instead riveted her to the doorjamb for a minute, then drew her inside.

The room was darkened because the blinds were halfway down, but she could still see the two cribs placed on opposite sides of the room. They were hospital cribs, bare metal slats with little decoration. A clear Lucite wall about a foot high ran around the inside to keep the infants' hands from protruding as they slept. But what was even more innovative was the top, a contraption also made out of Lucite that was something like a cap on a pickup truck. It raised the headroom inside the crib about a foot but made it impossible for the children to climb out. Cages, Margaret thought immediately, like those she'd seen for transporting animals. What could be wrong with these children?

As her eyes got adjusted to the light she saw a baby sleeping in the crib on the left, and another, quite awake, in a blue stretchy on the other side. The child stopped crying and was just looking at her. Margaret took a step farther into the room and felt her heart stop. It was a beautiful little boy, with blue eyes and a face as perfectly formed as any on an Ivory Snow commercial. He pulled himself up and held out his hands through the bars to her, straining. Ten months, Margaret thought, maybe eleven. She came over and took hold of his tiny fingers.

"What's the matter?" she said in a soft voice and bent down to kiss him. She wanted to pick him up and hold him but there was no way she could see to open the contraption on top. As she straightened to look closer the baby began to cry again and clutched even harder at her hands. His little feet in the pajamas were trying to get on top of the Lucite screen, trying to get him higher so he could still see her.

"I'm not going away," she said, bending down again to look. But she didn't see a thing connected to him, no IV or respirator, or anything. The name on the little card taped to the side announced that this was Eric Williams but it didn't give any indication of his problem. Why was he in a darkened room in a city hospital with a dozen other babies? Margaret heard a scraping noise and turned around to see a different nurse standing in the doorway. Good, she thought, *she'll tell me*.

"What are you doing here?" the other woman asked in surprise. It wasn't really a challenge, but on the other hand, it wasn't one of the friendliest greetings Margaret had ever received. She ignored the question.

"What's wrong with these children? They look perfectly healthy to me."

"Oh, they are," the nurse said, coming in and sticking a toy stuffed fish inside the crib with baby Eric. "Healthy as you and me. Healthier than any of the new babies down on obstetrics." She stuck her hand inside and made the fish swim up the little boy's leg up to his tummy. He looked curiously at the little toy and smiled. She wiggled it and this time he giggled. He stuck his hand out to touch it.

"So why are they here?" Margaret asked, frowning. She ran through the possibilities in her head. AIDS infected, quarantined, allergic . . .

"Parents didn't want them, or maybe they just couldn't be bothered to take care of them. One or two are abused." The nurse just shrugged but Margaret felt a weight like a heavy stone settle on her heart. Her hand went up to her chest.

"Didn't want them!" she repeated. She looked over at the baby in the blue stretchy. He was now batting the stuffed fish against the crib bars. "But then how long will they stay here?" Margaret pressed.

"Until they can find foster parents for them. Unfortunately, it's not a short process. This one, for example, Eric, came in at a year. He's now fifteen months old."

"He's here three months like this?" Margaret looked around the room incredulously. "No toys, no place to walk."

"Some toys, and every day we get a few volunteers to come in and play with them for an hour. I thought you might have been one of them."

"Three months?" Margaret repeated.

"Samantha over there has been here four months." This time it was the nurse's turn to look doubtful. "You never heard the expression 'boarder babies'? Been in all the papers."

"I had no idea . . ." Margaret began then turned back to Eric. "It's such a shame."

"It sure is, honey, but now if you're not a volunteer you're not supposed to be here. You want to volunteer, you gotta go down to Volunteer Services in the lobby to sign up. Either way, I'm afraid you gotta go. With ten screaming kids I got my hands full."

"Volunteer," Margaret said adamantly. "I'll do more than that." She turned and angrily pushed her way out into the corridor.

Two

APRIL WAS A GOOD MONTH ON THE Broadway benches. February's frozen and encrusted snow had long since melted and the first little tulip buds were poking up next to the subway gratings on the islands. With the warmer weather the streets got busier, which made the pleasant pastime of people-watching more rewarding. While things were constantly changing around the avenue—new luxury apartment skyscrapers going up over two-story warehouses, new multi-screen cinema complexes replacing old-fashioned revival houses, *nouvelle* cuisine restaurants squeezing out steak and beer joints—the character of the street remained intact. Broadway was the grande dame of the West Side, a little down at the heels but still full of energy and experience. Home to both saint and sinner, it was an avenue that in one block could take you strolling past two bag ladies and an equal number of Pulitzer Prize winners. If New York was a melting pot, then Broadway was its ladle. There was a rhythm to the street, a definite timing that saw the Wall Streeters hit the subway stations by seven-thirty, the waves of children on their way to school an hour later, then the shopkeepers followed by the nannies and moms out strolling their toddlers, and finally the serious shoppers heading down to Zabar's and Fairway. And this all before lunch. It was a large canvas but those who appreciated it the most were the regulars on the benches, the old-timers who had little else to do and fewer places to do it in. And of all the regulars, the ones who met each afternoon on the benches on the island at Eighty-second Street were by far its best students.

"Did you see that?" Berdie exclaimed, pointing in the direction of one of the stores. "Freudenheimer went and took down the sale on roasted chickens. Two ninety-five a pound last week and today up to four dollars." She shook a bony finger in the direction of the poultry shop. "Didn't I say nothing good would come of that new awning?" She looked at her friend Rena and frowned, the creases in her face deepening with her expression. "You won't catch me buying a chicken there again."

"Ha," Rena chuckled. "The last chicken you bought was during the Truman administration. Don't kid me." She bent over and removed the rubber band from one of her stockings. She rummaged on her wrist until she found one slightly larger, then bent back down and replaced it. "That's better," she said filing the first rubber band back on her wrist. "Leastwise, *I* never found out about any chicken made it inside your kitchen," she added pointedly.

"Didn't I have you up last week for Sid's seventy-sixth?" Berdie asked with a note of asperity. "Don't complain."

"Big deal, Twinkies and ginger ale. I can get that at the center." Rena leaned back into the bench and nodded in the direction of the other bench across the intersection. "You still not talking to Durso, I see. It's been over a week."

"I should talk to that old Bolshevik. I'll rot in hell before I say another word to him."

Rena sighed. "It was only a little cayenne pepper in with the crumbs."

"Behind my back. That man's got a mean sense of humor and all because he flunked out of the Lincoln Brigade."

"So what harm did it do? Pigeons can't sneeze."

"What harm!" Berdie sounded incredulous. "After all these years you've known me, seen me feeding them, you ask what harm . . ."

"Well," Rena shrugged. "Durso apologized."

"Big deal. Like he apologized for backing the Soviets when they invaded Hungary in fifty-six. Apologies ain't going to get me back Trundles who won't go near me he's so mad, or Sham Sham. Poor bird's eyes are still so crossed she's bumping into things and won't touch a crumb I throw her. That little joke cost me a third of my flock."

Rena leaned closer to her friend. "Listen dear, New York

has a lot of shortages, but pigeons ain't one of them. Another week from now you won't even miss them. Durso's been your friend as long as I have."

"Some friend." Berdie stole a glance across the intersection at the three men who were chatting. Durso, of course, was dressed in his ubiquitous tweed blazer with the elbow patches, his combined shield and croix de guerre for over thirty years in the city public school system. From far away you couldn't see its many tiny burn marks, left by the years of pipe smoking. Not that Pancher Reese, the gentleman to his left, looked more elegant. His sweater boasted enough pulled threads to make him resemble some human scouring pad. The third man, by contrast, was dressed neatly in a houndstooth jacket and slacks. His white hair was combed back neatly and his shoes, even from thirty feet away, shone in the afternoon sun.

"See that," Berdie said. "Sid's just had a new haircut and polish. Means he's going to be insufferable later on. Must have been at least an exacta."

Rena shrugged. "Coulda been the daily double. He's getting more generous with himself since his birthday. What the hell, he loses enough."

"Either way, we're in for a lecture on his uncanny ability to pick nags." She gathered her bag of crumbs and pocketbook and started to get up. "Durso's bad enough; throw in Sid's self-righteousness and it's just too much. I think I'll head on over to the center."

Before she had a chance to get off the bench, Rena placed a hand on her arm. "I almost forgot. Margaret called me this morning and asked me to meet her here. She wanted to tell me something. I think she also wants to tell the others."

Berdie sat back down. "About what?"

"I don't know," Rena smiled and pointed. "But you won't have long to find out. Here she comes now."

Getting everyone together took a little doing. Enough space had to be negotiated from a few of the transients on Berdie's island, then the three men had to be coaxed across the intersection. But Margaret doggedly made the effort and in five minutes they were all seated and looking at her radiant face. Sid, not shy with his ad hominems, broke the ice first.

"You want to tell us what's lighting you up like a Roman candle? Last time I saw you this excited was when you got the full bingo card at Saint Ignatius."

Margaret looked at each of her five friends in turn. A playful smile was dancing across the corners of her mouth and her seventy-two-year-old eyes were brighter than those of any auditioning chorus girl.

"I thought you'd all like to know," she finally said, "that I'm about to become a mother."

A truck sounded a blast on its horn half a block away but it made not the slightest impression on the five listeners. Under the circumstances, the launching of an antiballistic missile from Freudenheimer's poultry store across the street would have drawn about the same response.

"A what?" Rena finally breathed.

"A mother," Margaret repeated, "you know, as in rock-a-bye-baby . . ."

"I think we are all aware of what a mother is," Durso interrupted. "I think Rena was simply registering shock in its applicability to you." He pulled out his pipe and thrust it into his mouth. "I know they are doing some crazy things with biogenetics, but surely they haven't yet made the breakthrough to geriatric obstetrics." He pulled out a match and tried to light whatever remained of the bottle inside the briar.

"Besides," Sid added. "You look slimmer than ever." He elbowed Pancher in the side but the retired tailor wouldn't even grace him with a chuckle. Knowing his friend Margaret to be usually quite literal, what Pancher said was, "What the hell are you talking about?"

"I'm getting a baby to come stay with me." Margaret said. "What's so strange about that? After mothering all of you the past ten years, it's about time I did it for real."

"A kitten?" Berdie asked hopefully.

"No, a real live, crawling, screaming, little person . . . a human person." She looked around again at the blank faces. "You know, a b-a-b-y . . ."

"Can I ask," Durso interrupted, "where you came to acquire said baby? A relative die?"

"Nope, I volunteered to take one in. I'm going to be a foster mother."

Giving a name to it dispelled some of her friends' confusion. It didn't, however, do a thing to dent their disbelief.

"But Margaret," Rena asked, "Where you gonna keep it? Babies need things—prams, cribs, changing tables."

"And diapers," Sid added.

"It will be an effort," Margaret agreed, "but if you could have only seen these poor children at the hospital, all quite healthy, just longing for someone to love them. Besides, what else do I have to do? One day with the book cart is fine, but the other six days, being an old lady with the rest of you," she shook her head, "arguing the fine points of Marxism as it applies to the price of chopped chuck at Sloan's . . . it's not a role I'm suited for."

"Well, I think you're crazy," Durso said. "A seventy-two-year-old widow taking in an infant!" He tapped his pipe on the bench next to him to make his point.

"You're just like Oscar," Margaret said coldly. "Always afraid of something outside the party line. I suppose that's why we never had kids all those years. But it's never too late. What makes me, a survivor in this city since before Prohibition, less able to care for an infant than some sixteen-year-old high school dropout?"

"Certifiable," Sid said and punched out his racing form. He bent over it to study what was doing at Monmouth.

Margaret shook her head. "Of course, I could use some help."

Berdie reached out and touched her friend's hand. "You mean you already have the little baby?"

"They tell me it takes some time," Margaret said. "You got to be investigated and approved. I won't get him until May."

"Him?" Berdie pressed. "Who?"

"Baby Eric. The one that got me thinking about the whole thing. They tell me he'll probably still be available." Margaret looked at them soberly.

"Well, count me out," Sid said. "I never changed a diaper in my life and I don't intend to start now that I'm finally entering my golden years."

"More like leaden," Margaret shot back. "Come on, give

the kid a break. He could use a solid father figure. How about you, Pancher?"

"Well, I don't know." Pancher reached up and scratched behind an ear. "Can't say I'm really too interested. Arthritis is acting up with all the rain."

"It won't be raining in May."

He just looked back at her and shook his head. "The fact is, I don't know anything about babies, Margaret. The closest I ever got was when the Park Avenue ladies came into my tailoring shop. The kids they dragged in were always pulling at things, unrolling, unzipping, tearing. Made me nervous." He looked down guiltily at his hands hooked into the bottom of his fraying suspenders.

"And Joe, you of course are too busy?" Margaret continued.

Durso looked up and nodded. "You know I am writing a book on capitalism's failure in public education."

"Yes, how could I forget. You've been working on it for fifteen years now."

"I don't see how I could spare the time . . ."

"No, of course not." Margaret sighed and got up. "Well, I can see this is not getting me anywhere."

"Wait," Berdie said. "I might be able to help. Could collect some toys for the little baby at least."

Margaret looked at the other woman and leaned over. "Thanks, dear. You always had a good heart underneath that sweater, which for some reason is always buttoned wrong." She redid the two top buttons so the collar lay flat.

"Practicing already," Durso said.

Margaret shot him a black look and stood back up.

"It's so nice having such good, helpful friends, the kind you can always rely on." She looked them over again. "Makes me want to move to Anchorage." She turned on her heels and walked across the street as the light changed. Fortunately the driver of the beer truck spotted her out of the corner of his eye and slammed on his brakes. A string of curses followed her across the intersection but Margaret never broke stride. She couldn't remember when she'd been so angry.

Three

IT TOOK THREE WEEKS TO GET APPROVED by the agency that was in charge of baby Eric, three weeks in which Margaret thought every day about the poor child languishing in his tiny crib. Every morning she went to visit and play with him, and every afternoon she made attempts to transform her tiny apartment into a nursery. She was appalled at how long it took to pry Eric free. But her name had to be run through some computer in Albany to check that she didn't have a record for child abuse, then she had to have letters of recommendation sent, then a health check, then neighbors had to be interviewed. Only then could an investigator make a visit to her house. By that time she had already traded the dark and somber still lifes on her wall, the ones Oscar had loved so much, for some big teddy bear posters and a colorful quilt top she had been saving. She had gotten the superintendent to give her a fresh coat of paint finally. And for ten dollars extra and all the coffee the painter could drink, she had gotten it a light aqua rather than the ubiquitous rental white. Margaret had put colorful ribbons up over the place where the crib was to go, and on the wall next to it, some animal pictures painstakingly cut out of a children's magazines. All in all, she figured, her apartment would look rather cheerful to a fifteen-month-old. The big ticket items, the crib and changing tables, she was still working on, tracing down a lead to a relatively new set through her nephew in New Jersey.

The social worker, a twenty-five-year-old gum-chewing woman with sneakers and a sweatshirt that said ''Property of Alçatraz,'' took one look around and frowned.

''Where's the smoke detector?'' was the first thing she said.

Margaret winced. *Where the hell was it,* she thought painfully. She recalled the super saying something about one last year, but where did he put it?

''In the hallway,'' she said finally. ''Outside the bedroom.'' *Please let it be there*, she prayed as she led the other woman to the spot she hoped it might be.

''Change the battery regularly?'' the younger woman said, looking up at the round plastic unit.

''Every six months or so,'' Margaret said, crossing her fingers behind her back. The woman bent down and checked something off on a clipboard that had materialized out of her briefcase.

''Mind if I look around?'' she asked.

''Go ahead, please.'' Margaret opened the door to the bedroom and stepped back. She took a furtive glance up at the smoke detector and waited for the woman to return. In a minute she was back with a look on her face that made Margaret uneasy.

''Anything the matter?'' she asked.

''Have a seat,'' the woman said. ''I have to ask you some questions.'' Up came the clipboard and the other woman began the interrogation, checking things off as she went. Besides wanting a thorough chronology of her life, she also asked about Margaret's current health (even though she had just been through an agency-mandated checkup), the reason she and her husband had never had children, her reasons for living alone, the number of packs of cigarettes she smoked a day, whether she professed to any particular religion, and finally, if she ever considered having extramarital affairs.

''I don't really think that's applicable to a seventy-two-year-old widow,'' Margaret smiled awkwardly. ''In fact, in the context of this investigation, I'm not sure that it's even applicable to a twenty-five-year-old newlywed. I just want to get little Eric out of that hospital cage. I don't understand all the rest of this stuff. Does it really matter how religious I am to change his diaper?''

The social worker gave her a frosty look and put her clipboard away.

"Mrs. Binton, under the circumstances here, I'm afraid I can't approve you to be a foster parent."

Margaret felt her hands clench. She looked around for her handbag and the package of Camels. She had to do something with her hands or she was afraid they might take it upon themselves to strangle the little officious twit.

"And why is that?" she managed after lighting the cigarette.

"No window guards. We can't approve any household without child window guards."

"Don't you think you could have mentioned that before our friendly half-hour interview?"

"Well I have these forms to fill . . ."

"Is that the only problem?"

The other woman nodded.

Margaret got up and walked to the newly painted intercom on the wall by the front door. In a few seconds she had the doorman on the line. "Harry, could you send up Spyros, please, right away." She replaced the earphone and came back to the living room. "I'm going to make us a nice cup of tea," she said, regaining her composure. "And then you're going to wait while my superintendent installs as many window guards as you want. And then you're going to put down that my apartment meets all your agency's requirements to receive a foster child. I'm sure you don't mind waiting another half hour or so . . . of your time."

"Well, I . . ."

"Good, now how do you like your tea, cream or lemon?"

Four

MRS. HELEN REGENCY LOOKED AT THE APplication on her desk and rubbed the side of her nose. It was a gesture she found comforting when she had to think. She rubbed and rubbed and tried to imagine what a seventy-two-year-old widow wanted with a little baby boy. More specifically, she wondered what she wanted with this particular little boy, since she had mentioned his name in her application. How—what was it, Mrs. Binton?—had even found out about him was a mystery since the names of all of the agency's boarder babies were supposed to be confidential. But Mrs. Regency was not new at this and understood that the bureaucracy in the city's children services agencies was a web of such inefficient and careless design as almost to ensure the occurrence of the unexpected and unwanted. Not that this application was particularly a bad thing, just interesting. Mrs. Regency rubbed harder and opened a special file she had on her desk. As the Youth Benevolent Association's director of foster-care placement, it was her duty to match the children her organization had accepted or been persuaded to accept by the city with their list of potential volunteer foster parents. On the surface, such a collating appeared straightforward. In reality, it was probably as difficult as figuring out a guest list for a Papal visit to Tel Aviv. First and foremost, there simply were not enough foster parents. And, if by some miracle, the number of children to be placed dropped low enough to equal the number of available beds, then the children, or the parents, were somehow wrong for each other. After ten years as a social worker, she knew the bottlenecks by heart. Few foster parents wanted older children, fewer still wanted siblings, and finding anyone to take in a physically or mentally handicapped child was almost impossible. Then there were those who wanted only pre-adoptive children. But still the kids came, by the thousands every year, victims of neglect, abuse, or the simple inability of their parents to provide food and shelter. It began with drugs, alcohol, and poverty and ended in a folder on Helen Regency's desk, or folders, because there were two of them. One was for the children who were emergency cases, who needed immediate removal and help; the other was for long-term cases whose parents were not capable of caring for them now or possibly ever. That final distinction was not made by anyone at her agency. But Mrs. Regency kept an informal list of those children who she suspected would be adoptable, whose parents were either dead, permanently gone, fogged out on drugs, or so abusive that their rights would be terminated by the court. That was her special folder, and that was the one Eric fit into. But even in that folder, Eric was special. Eric was white.

Not that Mrs. Regency had anything against black, Hispanic, Mexican, or even Third World children. She herself was a child of a black Detroit auto worker and a light-skinned Alabama elementary school teacher, and all her friends were black. It was just that a healthy, young, single, white, adoptable child was something of a rarity . . . and now this widow, Mrs. Binton, wanted to be his foster mother.

Under normal conditions she'd never let that happen. She had a long list of prospective adoptive parents for Eric. But what she needed was another month until the court hearing, until Jason Sawyer, the agency lawyer, could establish that parental rights had been terminated. Then she could go to the set of parents she chose and say definitely that he was adoptable. Right now Eric was a little too much in limbo. The judges were sometimes crazy. One gets up, fights with his wife, and the rest of the day terminates all rights. Another sees an uplifting old rags-to-riches film the night before and decides to continue a remand for another six months in the hopes the parents will pull together. Who could figure it? Not the pre-adoptive parents, that's the last thing they wanted. So she needed another month or so on Eric and besides the city was pressing the Youth Benevolent Association to take him after the three months he had spent in the hospital . . . She rubbed her nose now with the other hand. Maybe Mrs. Binton would be just right. A warm, caring, grandmotherly type who would be more than happy to take care of a little child for a month or so. After the court hearing she could always send Eric to another set of parents. That was part of the agreement all foster parents signed. Basically they had no rights until after a year. Binton knew that. What could go wrong? She took Eric's papers out of the file and matched it with Margaret's. Then she signed her approval form and put everything in an envelope to go upstairs. That done, she felt a lot better. She glanced at her watch and noticed that it was getting on to four o'clock. The aerobics class at her health club started at four-thirty, so she put her folders away, tidied up her desk, and left the office. If there was one thing she couldn't do without, it was her health club. It took away all the tensions of her difficult job.

Five

THE LITTLE DEAR HAD TO HAVE NEW PAjamas, didn't he, Margaret thought. Those things they gave him in the hospital looked like a mini version of an intern's scrub suit. They were probably as uncomfortable as they were unstylish. And some new undershirts and a small blanket. And, of course, she needed some bottles. The hospital said they'd give her some when she picked Eric up but she wanted to start fresh. And maybe, if it wasn't too expensive, a stroller. She had to admit, the pram she got from her nephew did look a little too small for Eric. She waited impatiently for the clerk in Bob's Babyland to finish his sale and wait on her.

Now what in tarnation was this little device? Margaret fingered the seat that broke down to a changing mat, that doubled as a trampoline toy, that could also be used as a chest carrier, or at the very least, a handy bag for diapers. By the time she finished reading the options and instructions, she was so confused she turned to something she knew. She collected four new glass bottles and turned back to the clerk.

"I think I'm going to go with the ones with collapsible bags myself," a young woman said next to her. "All my friends tell me they're easier. I don't know anyone that uses those bottles anymore."

"Bags?" Margaret looked surprised. "You mean when it's time for bed you give the baby a bag?" Margaret was truly confused.

The other lady, eight months pregnant and with the confident expression of a Raphael Madonna, nodded. "No cleanup, and less work."

"I'm just old fashioned, I guess," Margaret said. "I've always liked glass. What's that thing?" Margaret pointed to the box in the other woman's hand.

"Breast pump."

"Pump?" Margaret looked down at the other woman's breasts which, to her, looked quite adequate.

"For expressing milk if you're going to be away."

"Oh." Margaret's face turned red. "I see."

"Your daughter will know," the woman said airily. "A lot of things have changed since you gave birth. She taking breathing classes?"

Something else to worry about, Margaret thought. *Now you had to go to school to learn how to inhale to be a mother?*

"No," Margaret said. "In fact I don't have a daughter. All this stuff is for me."

The other woman looked at all the clothes and the blanket and bottles and after some time gave up trying to put it together.

"I'm taking in a little foster baby," Margaret helped.

"Oh, isn't that nice," the pregnant woman said, but of course now that she realized they were talking apples and bananas there was no way the conversation was going to last. She turned away and started poking around the carseat display. At that moment the clerk started ringing up Margaret's purchases. When he was finished he looked up and asked, "Got everything you need?"

"Well, in fact, I was wondering about strollers. Perhaps you could help me pick one out."

A smile came across the clerk's face like he'd just won the lottery and he stepped around the counter. "They're over here," he said. "All twelve models. Of course, they all have different features."

She had to stop him ten minutes later as he was still explaining that the Aprica had a double clutch brake and six different reclining positions and went down into a full sleep bed, which then could be used as a carrying basket for infants, while the MacLaren, weighing in at slightly over twenty pounds, doubled as a car seat and had shock absorbers in its underframe as well as a sunshade with options for an enclosed pod for inclement weather—or that the Italian Inglesina, which was truly European in styling, came in a wide selection of colors and was psychologically more suitable in that parent and child faced each other. . . .

"Excuse me," Margaret interrupted. "These sound like formula-one race cars. All I'm looking for is something that will roll a little boy of fifteen months and folds up for the bus. Preferably for under twenty dollars."

Deflated, the clerk gestured toward something in a corner that looked like a folded-up umbrella. "Twenty-three ninety-five," he said.

"Perfect, I'll take it," Margaret replied and handed him some cash.

When the clerk was finished and Margaret was on her way out, the other woman hove into view around the wall of cribs.

"Good luck," Margaret shouted. "Hope you get what you want."

"Oh I am," the pregnant woman said. "It's a boy . . . his name is Andrew." She held up a little shirt she was buying with an "A" on it.

"Science," Margaret grumbled on her way through the doors. "Next they'll be getting their IQs before birth."

Six

"AND WHO MIGHT THIS BE?" HARRY SAID through the cigar wedged in his mouth. He was peering over his glasses, finger still pointing to the last word he had read in Mike Lupica's column on the Yankees. The idea that he might actually get up and help open the front door had never crossed his mind in the ten years he had been the doorman of Margaret's building. As far as he was concerned, his job was one of security, which meant answering the intercom and giving everyone the eyeball when they came in. Except in December, of course, when he was miraculously on his feet, helping with packages, pushing the self-service elevator button for tenants, even opening the door in anticipation of his harvest of holiday remembrances. But today was April 20 and any kind of greeting from Harry occasioned mild surprise.

"This is Eric," Margaret said proudly. "He's coming to live with me."

Harry leaned forward and peered into the little boy's face. "He's cute enough. Where'd you get him?"

"Macy's, Harry, in the children's department."

"Very funny."

"Mail come yet?"

"Nope. What do you want, it's only three in the afternoon." He leaned back over the paper. "He be staying long?"

"I hope so. Say hello to the man, Eric. Harry can teach you a lot about baseball." Eric was struggling to put a sock in his mouth, but he did stop long enough to give Harry a grin that featured a lone tooth as its focal point.

"Pretty good," Harry said and went back to Lupica's analysis of the Yankees' hitting. "Good luck with him."

"Thanks," Margaret said and continued upstairs.

"Now listen," Margaret said to Eric later that afternoon. "You've been very good. You ate all your food and you've been polite to everyone. But I think it's about time you learned how to walk. Fifteen months . . . it's time already."

The baby sat in the middle of the living-room floor and looked at his new foster mother as if she were some big stuffed doll. He smiled at her but had no idea what she was saying.

"Here, let me show you." She bent down and stood him up. "You're no longer in a hospital bed, you're free. Take a step."

Eric fell on his fanny.

"Try again," she said and propped him up, this time next to the couch. He held on for a moment, looked both ways, then cruised a few steps to the right. When he got to the end of the couch, he looked back at her for instructions. "Take a step," Margaret urged again and held her hands out.

Piece of cake, Eric must have thought, and stepped lively. This time he picked himself up off his elbows and looked at her in bewilderment.

"That's a good start," she said. "You'll have it in a week. Now, how about we get you to say a few words." She looked at his tiny body. "*Pupik*, can you say *pupik*?" She waited. Eric grinned and pulled himself up again next to the couch. This time he explored to the other end.

"*Pupik*," Margaret repeated.

Nothing. "Maybe that's too hard. How about this, can you say *m-a-m-a*? Mama."

Eric looked at her carefully because now he realized this woman was serious. His tiny mouth rounded and out came the sound "*oma*."

Margaret wanted to cry. "Yes, Moma," she said and laughed.

"Oma," Eric said again and Margaret felt as if her heart would explode.

Seven

THE NEXT DAY, ON THE WAY TO CENTRAL Park, Margaret decided to introduce Eric to her friends. Being that it was still early, only Berdie and Rose Gaffery were in attendance on the Eighty-second street bench, Berdie dishing out her morning handfuls of crumbs to the local birds and Rose trying to consolidate six of her shopping bags into five. The two of them looked as if they were auditioning for a part in some street-life sitcom. Rose's ripped stockings were rolled down to her ankles, her three layers of sweaters were misbuttoned, and her hair was being held in check by a ripped napkin from one of the local fish restaurants. Berdie, never one to be concerned with style or size, had a dress that hung off her like a parachute stuck on a tree. Neither looked up until Margaret pushed her way between them.

''My goodness,'' Berdie said. ''It's a real baby.''

''What's this,'' Rose said, squinting first at the stroller and then at Margaret. In her hand she still held the inside of a toaster iron, which she was trying to cram into a Bloomingdale's bag. Between her feet was a copy of an Italian magazine, *Oggi Sardegna,* which was apparently the next thing to be stuffed.

''His name is Eric,'' Margaret said. ''He arrived yesterday.''

''I like that name,'' Rose said. ''They told me you was getting one, but I don't see how you did it.''

''It wasn't easy,'' Margaret said and lit a cigarette. ''What with the bureaucracy at Special Services, and the confusion at the Youth Benevolent Association, I'm surprised he's sitting where he is. Can you imagine, three months in a hospital and when I arrived to check him out they couldn't release him until he had a medical checkup. Took another three hours before they found a doctor to do it. Three more hours in that cage of his. And guess what, the doctors at the YBA don't trust the city doctors, which means I have to bring him in for a completely new physical tomorrow over on the East Side.'' She inhaled deeply on the cigarette. ''And that's only the beginning. He's got a schedule of shots and home visits that'll make sure he never gets another midday nap.''

''Still,'' Rose said, ''it's a baby. You suppose they'd let me have a baby?''

Margaret laughed. ''I don't think the Youth Benevolent Association would approve of your accommodations, Rose, although quite frankly, they're probably healthier for a baby than being stuck in a cage. Lots of exercise and fresh air anyway.''

''I suppose not,'' Rose said softly.

''But I certainly could use your help.'' Margaret said. ''Everyone else seems to be overburdened.''

''Really?'' Rose beamed. ''Now that would be something.'' She thought a moment and looked down at her bags. ''Hey, let's see if I still got it here.'' She drove down into one shopping bag, rummaged through layers of papers, old clothing, and batteries, then finally withdrew her hand. In it was a little stuffed monkey with its tail half ripped off. ''I was going to sew it back on,'' she said. ''But I never found the time. Now I got a reason.'' She rummaged inside another bag and found a needle and some thread.

''How you ever find anything in there is a wonder,'' Berdie said.

''I've got my system,'' Rose said proudly as she stitched. ''Ain't anything I got I can't find. There,'' she said after another minute, ''good as new.'' She bent over and placed it in Eric's lap. The little boy looked at it for a minute, picked it up by its lopsided tail, and handed it back to Rose.

''He doesn't want it?'' She sounded hurt.

''I think it's a game,'' Margaret said. ''Hand it back.'' She did and this time Eric looked more closely at the monkey. He took his finger and poked it in the eye.

''Cute as a button,'' Berdie said.

''Rose, if you want to come,'' Margaret said finally, ''we're going to the park. The fumes here would choke a Welsh coal miner. Funny I never noticed it before." She got up and grabbed the handles of the stroller. Without hesitation, Rose took hold of the five bags and stood up behind her.

"The park?" Berdie said softly.

Margaret looked over her shoulder. "Central Park. It's where you take babies for fresh air . . ."

Berdie looked a little embarrassed but she said it anyway, "Mind if I come too?"

Margaret grinned. "Not at all," she said. "I'd be delighted." She looked down at Eric. "I mean, we'd be delighted."

The three women and the little baby pushed into the playground at Eighty-fifth Street and were immediately attacked by a five-year-old on a GI Joe tricycle. He wheeled past them twice, firing his imaginary nose cannon, and announced that they were all dead. His foray completed, he went on another search and destroy mission toward a group of Irish au pair girls pushing their charges on the tire swings.

"Dangerous place," Margaret laughed and unstrapped Eric by the sand box. She lifted him into it then sat down on the wooden rim. Rose and Berdie flanked her and together they watched Eric joyfully grab fistfuls of sand and throw them at his feet.

"He needs a shovel," Berdie said, "and a pail." Cautiously, she edged over to a set she spotted nearby, picked them up, and brought them back to the little boy. "There," she said proudly. "What's a sandbox without the proper tools?" She smiled shyly at Margaret.

They continued to watch little Eric in silence but after a while Margaret let her gaze wander. The playground was full of toddlers and preschoolers with about as many nannies, mothers, housekeepers, and au pairs. Unlike their charges, the caretakers seemed to divide themselves into separate homogenous groups. Mothers talked to other mothers or read, black West Indian housekeepers laughed and joked with friends in the same patois, white-uniformed nannies chatted together but kept a stern watchful eye out for their little dears, and the Irish au pairs, combining business with pleasure, were in there on all fours, mixing it up in the sand with their kids or pushing swings while they talked about boyfriends Brian or Dennis or Sean.

"Seems like there's no one for us," Margaret observed. "Where are all the grandmas?"

"Maybe they got the day off for good behavior," Berdie said.

"Here, you stop that," Rose shouted. She got up and advanced into the sandbox where the GI Joe marauder was now shooting a cap gun at little Eric.

"Don't frighten him," she said.

He turned the gun and pointed it at Rose. "Bam, bam, bam; die, Cobra Commander," the little savage hissed.

"I'll Cobra Commander you," Rose said and raised one of the bags she was still clutching. The little boy took one look and ran screaming back across the playground. His housekeeper glanced his way but didn't think it was important enough to disengage herself. In another minute the kid was back on his trike terrorizing another part of the playground.

"Sure beats the boring old bench on Eighty-second," Margaret said. She bent down and brushed a little sand off Eric's socks. "What do you suppose Sid and Durso and the others are doing now?"

"I don't know," Berdie said. "But it can't be half as much fun."

In fact, Sid and Pancher, that very moment, were standing behind a large sycamore tree twenty yards away watching the goings-on in the playground. They had spotted the little group as it crossed Broadway and had followed them all the way to the park, pussyfooting around bushes and rocks so not to be spotted. The closest Sid had ever before come to a fifteen-month-old was on a train ride to Monmouth where, somewhere past Newark, the little devil had treated Sid to a close inspection of his previous meal. It wasn't that Sid didn't like babies, he just didn't understand them. Like now, for example. He wondered why anyone in their right mind would pile sand on their head and then pat it down with a shovel.

"What the hell are we doing here?" Pancher asked.

"I just wanted to see Margaret in action. I still don't believe it."

"Believe it," Pancher said. "She's done crazier things."

The two watched in silence for another minute. ''Look,'' Sid said finally. ''He's digging a hole.''

''So?''

''That's pretty good for a year old.''

''Fifteen months I hear.''

''Still, the kid's got talent.''

''Ah,'' Pancher said disgustedly. ''Let's go. I got better things to do than watch this.'' He turned around and nearly had a coronary. Five feet away was a city policeman watching them closely.

''Good morning gentlemen,'' the cop said. ''Can I ask what you might be doing behind this tree so intent on that playground?''

''Um, ah, officer,'' Sid pointed, ''That's my little grandson over there. Just pointing him out to my friend here.'' He smiled and took Pancher by the arm. ''We were just on our way to the bocce courts and made a little detour. Good day.''

''What'd he think we were?'' Pancher asked when they were out of earshot.

''I don't know,'' Sid answered. ''But I guarantee it wasn't nice.''

As popular as Eric had been with Berdie and Rose, he was an opening-night sensation at the Florence E. Bliss Senior Citizen's Center. He was the youngest thing to have passed through their doors since Mrs. Schwartzwalder brought her grandniece to portray a ribboned and diapered 1982 for a New Year's Day celebration. Even without a costume, Eric won every heart and eye that was not attuned to the pinochle and canasta tables—and even some that were. At three in the afternoon the place was crowded.

Rena Bernstein started by doing a little dance on Eric's tummy with her fingers. A self-professed ballerina in her youth, Rena loved music and listened to it constantly through her battered Walkman radio. But this afternoon she had taken out her earphones and choreographed her own recital on Eric's delightfully squirming body. His giggles filled the card and snack area of the downstairs meeting room. After a minute Rena stood back up, brushed a wisp of gray hair from her eye, and took a deep breath.

"A baby," she said. "I'd forgotten how wonderful they were. So much fun."

"Except when they're hungry," Margaret added, "or tired, or itchy, or a dozen other things. But you're right, dear, they are resilient. You fix what's troubling them and in five minutes, they're back gurgling at you. Not nearly as moody as the bunch of us."

"Moody?" Roosa the Juicer said, ambling over. He'd just had his two cups of afternoon coffee and was fairly coherent. "Who's moody?"

"Not you," Rena said sarcastically. "As long as there's a bottle in your hand."

He shrugged and turned his stooped back on Rena. "Women!" he said disgustedly, and took a step closer to the little boy. He looked at him carefully for a moment and a tiny smile began fighting to transform his lined face. "Hey, you know what?" he said finally. "He looks like an uncle of mine. Uncle Vanya from Brest-Litovsk."

"Give me a break," Margaret said.

"No, really. Same chin." He bent closer to observe the Slovakian chin closer. "Could be a long lost great-grand-nephew or something."

"Well, he's not going to wind up waiting tables at Ratner's like you did if that's what you have in mind." Margaret said. She addressed the several people around her. "Little Eric's going to be a doctor."

"Oy," Rena Bernstein said. "And over-bill Medicare for a living. Let him be an artist. He can starve but at least he'd have a wonderful life."

"So, your life was so wonderful?" Roosa asked. "Heart transplants have more stability."

"Coming from you, that's amusing. The last straight line I saw you walking had bread at the end of it."

"Children, children!" Margaret shouted. "You're scaring Eric. Maybe I should buy two more strollers."

The two friends looked sheepishly at each other.

"Some role models," Margaret added.

"Sorry," they both said and looked back at the little boy. "Don't you think he's dressed too warm?" another woman in the little group around Margaret said. "Here, let me open that sweater."

"Time for his bottle yet?" Berdie asked.

"Not yet, but I was thinking of letting him crawl around on the mat a little. Is Alice downstairs?"

"Do pigeons have wings?" Roosa said with a snort and nodded in the direction of the staircase. "But she'll be happy to share it, especially with someone who can show her how to touch her toes."

Margaret grinned as she lifted Eric out of his stroller and followed them down to the basement and the Florence E. Bliss exercise room.

Alice McIlvaney was indeed downstairs and on the mats, attempting to exercise. She was a big, full-hipped woman made even bigger by a red wig the size of a cheerleader's pom-pom. Below her shock of hair she had on a black leotard and pink tights. Calling her figure pear-shaped would have been generous, but then in Margaret's book, being anything more shapely than an eggplant at age sixty-five was an accomplishment. When they entered the exercise room she was struggling to touch her toes with her outstretched and very red fingernails. She was about a foot away and had as much hope of making contact as Hearns had against Sugar Ray Leonard.

"Oof," she said and grabbed some more air in an attempt to get closer. First one hand then the other. In the background a little tape recorder was spilling out Jane Fonda's voice in a cadence that bore no relationship to Alice McIlvaney's movements. In other surroundings one might have said Alice was merely studying a particularly expensive manicure.

"Well," Roosa said impishly, "pumping iron again, I see."

Alice stopped her exertions and squinted at the door. Without her glasses everything seemed fuzzy, but the voice was unmistakable. She didn't even bother to respond.

"Alice," Margaret said with a grin. "I brought you some company to exercise with." She placed Eric on the mat and stood back up to watch.

Alice leaned over to reach for her glasses. "Is that you, Margaret?" When she had the lenses on her nose she found herself staring at a little boy who was on all fours and looking intently at her knee. "What's this?" she said happily.

"A baby," Berdie supplied.

"I can see that," Alice said. "But whose?"

"For the moment Eric's mine," Margaret said. "Do you mind if I let him crawl around a little on the mat? He needs the exercise and it's nice and soft."

Without waiting for approval, Eric began to explore the far reaches of the mat. The room they were in was the size of a good-sized living room but had only a simple table along one wall and the exercise mat in the center of the floor. Because the elevator didn't go down into the basement, the room was never used for the center's other activities, since many of the people at the center were on canes, walkers, or in wheelchairs. In fact, the only one who ever bothered to walk down the steep flight on a regular basis was Alice and she used it for only an hour or so each afternoon.

Eric came to the edge of the mat and sat back on his haunches awaiting further instructions.

"Can he walk?" Alice asked.

Margaret shook her head.

"He looks old enough." Alice got up and moved to his side. She lifted him up, held a tiny hand, and started walking towards Margaret. Halfway across the mat she let go. Eric took two more steps before he realized the change, looked behind him in apparent wonder at what he'd done, tottered for a moment out of sheer fright, then continued gleefully towards Margaret. Four steps later he crashed into her outstretched arms.

"He did it," Berdie shouted. Margaret was hugging him as Alice came over to share in the mini-celebration.

"First time," Margaret said with a little tear in the corner of her eye. "Three months in a cage, and two days after they let him out he walks."

"Imagine that," Alice said with a grin. "Just imagine." Clearly she was delighted with her role in Eric's new accomplishment.

"And it's only the beginning," Margaret added. "Just wait."

"What?" Roosa said gruffly, "tomorrow it's aerobics?"

"Tomorrow?" she said softly. "Oh lord, tomorrow it's the world."

Eight

VICTOR LAZARRE WAS ANGRY. SUSAN WAS on his ass again and when she got like that she could make his life miserable. So miserable, in fact, that he couldn't concentrate on the business. It was April already, another DeBeers sight was coming soon, which meant a trip to London, hundreds of thousands of dollars worth of diamonds to inspect, and all his wife could think about was babies. Babies over breakfast coffee, babies over dessert at Lutèce—babies everywhere. It was getting out of hand. The poor woman was losing it and it was beginning to get embarrassing. Imagine, bringing it up over dinner with his South African agent's wife. How the hell could she help, export a little white Afrikaner instead of uncut rough?

Lazarre got up from his Louis XIV desk with its burnished green Moroccan leather top and paced over to the window. The view was magnificent. From forty stories in the sky, the ships plying up the Hudson River looked like little pieces on a game board. The late afternoon sun reflecting off the water gave a reticulated texture to the surface far below. Somewhere out there was a goddamn baby for them, but sonofabitch if he knew how to find it. Nothing was working.

It was never supposed to be easy, but two years . . . and the indignity and heartache along the way! Worse than his first trip to Charterhouse Street when he had to suck up to the British diamond merchants. Worse even than trying to get into the New York Athletic Club and being rejected. Worse, because Susan never stopped. There was only one New York Athletic

Club, she told him; there were thousands of babies to adopt. Sure, so where the hell were they?

He turned away and went to sit on the Regency couch the decorator had insisted he buy. Actually, it was four years if you started counting from the day the doctor told Susan she couldn't have any children. But the first two years were more leisurely, bringing up the subject of adoption, setting the ground rules, casually investigating the possibilities. Victor had insisted, sine qua non, on a healthy white baby. That was the rock upon which was anchored his acceptance to the whole uncomfortable idea of adoption. Nothing just a little bit off either, like a little Eurasian or light-skinned Mexican. It wasn't easy, but then again, they were offering the home of Victor Lazarre, president of Lazarre Incorporated and one of the richest diamond merchants in New York.

The two years began with the ads in the papers. Thank God there were no names. Papers like the *Schenectady Courier* or the *Providence Journal*, in Catholic towns where there might be pregnant teenagers unwilling or scared out of having abortions. Just a telephone number, unlisted of course, and then a lot of waiting for that one phone call. It was a joke. On the one hand he was taking out twenty-thousand-dollar half-page ads in the *Wall Street Journal* for his diamond portfolio investment fund, and on the other, little pokey twenty-five-dollar three-liners in places he wouldn't even fly over. And where had it gotten them?

Well, a baby. That was true. A healthy little boy with gray eyes and a smile that seemed to make it all worthwhile. But a smile that lasted only long enough for Susan to bond with the kid before his real mother changed her mind about the whole deal. He had only himself to blame. The lawyer suggested they stay in Indiana for a week to get the mother's signature and make it ironclad, but a week away from business he couldn't afford and Susan didn't want to stay alone. Hell, he had thought, making it ironclad from New York only took a month longer, and what could happen in four weeks that hadn't already happened in nine months? They flew home and got the phone call two weeks later.

And two false leads from the West Coast on babies that found homes with relatives. And the pregnant friend of a friend of their Irish maid who, for ten thousand dollars in "medical fees," would part with her little unborn who turned out to be, unexpectedly to everyone but the mother, part Hispanic.

And that's not even talking about the fun and games they had with the surrogacy program before the Mary Beth Whitehead decision sent everyone packing. Christ! Victor lay back on the couch and put his feet upon the gilded arm. What a rat's nest that had been. Even Susan had to admit that. Five unsuccessful months with a surrogate who couldn't get pregnant if she'd slept with the Americal Division . . . So, where did that leave them? More ads, more leads—and Helen Regency, whose phone call he'd just received. Well, he'd wait that one out too and hope Susan hadn't gone off the deep end by then. What had the social worker said, the hearing was in early May. One more month . . . after four years, why not? Maybe he'd take Susan to London with him. Take her mind off things. Victor sighed, got back up, and went over to his desk. Money was supposed to buy you anything, at least that's what he was raised thinking. He didn't like the delay.

Nine

WHY NOT—IT WAS ONLY MAYBE TEN books' worth of space little Eric took up on the cart. The idea of giving up her Thursday volunteer work at the hospital was difficult for her to imagine after so many years. Her solution was simple; prop old Eric up somewhere between Mysteries and Romance and take him along for the ride. It was a solution that made everyone happy. Eric loved being wheeled along at eye level with Margaret and the attention he got at every stop, and the patients flipped when they saw the latest bibliophile in their midst. Together they went bouncing through the renal and pulmonary ward, the coronary care unit, and wound up this particular Thursday in late April in the osteopathic section, floor ten, talking to Peter Ryker, journalist and reformed skier.

"So where do you change his diaper?" Ryker said. bouncing Eric on his good knee.

"On your bed if you're not careful."

"He looks like one happy kid," Ryker said, lifting him back onto a flat part of the bed. He angled the television toward the little boy and punched a few buttons. His leg was down from traction but was still in a cast. "You did a wonderful thing there, Margaret."

"Oh, I don't know. I think I'm benefiting almost as much as Eric. If it weren't for all the red tape." Margaret shook her head. "Fact is, if I didn't put my foot down, I wouldn't be here today. That social worker wanted another visit but I just told her Thursday was my special day and it would have to wait. I expect she'll be angry when I arrive tomorrow, but can you imagine—dictating when I have to come in? I'm the one giving Eric a home and they're treating me like some minimum-wage employee.''

"Still, you've got him. My wife and I have been trying for years to have one. Looks like now we'll have to start thinking about adopting.'' He gave Eric a little tickle under the arm and leaned back into his pillow. "So why do they want to see him anyway?'' Ryker asked. "Examine for cigarette burns?''

"I suppose, but what bothers me is that the people there don't have the foggiest idea about children. They're just pushing folders around. The last time I went, this Mrs. Regency asked me how I was coming with Eric's toilet training. Fifteen months and they want me to start training him already! It's crazy.''

Eric shrieked and pointed to Ryker's television set and the big yellow creature most of America knows as Big Bird.

"Who's that?'' Margaret asked.

"I guess you don't let him watch television.''

"Don't have television. Got mystery books and crosswords.''

Ryker laughed. "God, Margaret, you are an anachronism.''

"Thanks. So, how about a book today? I'm afraid Eric replaced the sports section.''

"Hey, I forgot to tell you.'' Ryker sat up higher in bed. "Dr. Stillman gave me the green light to go home this afternoon.''

"That's great news.'' Margaret took his hand between hers. "Although I'll be sorry to see you go I'm sure your wife will be happy to have you back.''

Ryker leaned over and removed something from the top drawer of his night stand. "Here's my card at the paper. Let me show you around sometime.''

"Thank you, Peter.'' She bent down and lifted Eric back up to his spot on the cart. "I'll be looking for your stories. You go out and get them in Staten Island.''

Ryker laughed. "That's cold by now. I've got to look for something new. But hell, this is a big city, a million stories, right? I'll find me one.''

Ten

THE YOUTH BENEVOLENT ASSOCIATION was housed in a building on West Forty-ninth Street that originally had been the parish house of a nearby church. The church had long been torn down for its corner plot, but the parish house remained, wedged in between a parking lot and a taxicab garage. It was, as locations went, not the safest for little children. The building itself was sizable and with enough traffic to require a guard at the front door. Given the state of noise and energy from the kids in the lobby, it was not immediately clear whether his duty was to keep people out, or children in. Margaret told the receptionist whom she wanted to see, then took a seat in a corner.

About eight kids, all under the age of ten, were playing on the floor with plastic trucks, jet airplanes, toy soldiers, dolls, stuffed animals, and one very noisy imitation lawnmower. Surrounding them and seated along three walls were an equal number of grown-ups, presumably their parents. There was very little interchange between the children and their parents or among the parents themselves. The only ones who seemed to get it together were the kids who were having a good time playing and sharing the center's toys. Occasionally there was a misunderstanding, at which point a parent would try to resolve it, but generally the system worked well. The system, Margaret knew, was the nine to ten o'clock parent visitation, when foster parents relinquished their child to the loving company of a biological parent. Banished from the room, the foster parents sulked at a nearby coffee shop on Ninth Avenue while the biological parents spent the hour in the presence of their kids, thus maintaining their legal rights for yet another few months.

Fortunately for Margaret, Eric's parents were out of the picture. His mother was dead from a heroin overdose and his father was unknown. No one had presented himself at the hospital where Eric had been brought after his mother's death to claim the little boy, nor had Eric's mother indicated in the appropriate spot on the birth certificate a year earlier who his father was.

So Eric was not encumbered by the machinery of a legal system bent on reuniting parent and child. He was not encumbered by a parent willing to show up occasionally at visitations, who then disappeared like a ghost into a separate life. Nor was he encumbered by a host of relatives who insisted on his God-given rights as a citizen of New York's welfare society but who were too busy to offer him a home themselves. The only problems he was facing were in regard to the Youth Benevolent Association, which, as Margaret was fast discovering, could be quite as formidable.

Like for instance, the fact that it was maybe ninety degrees inside the lobby and all the windows and doors were shut. Regulations, she figured, keep the children toasty warm.

In five minutes, Mrs. Regency stepped out of the elevator. She came over with a face set with frown lines that looked as permanently etched as a biker's tattoo. Her hair was spiraled on the top of her head in a hairdo that would have made Tina Turner envious. Her small eyes were made even smaller by a pair of penciled eyebrows that resembled the McDonald's trademark. She was, in short, some piece of work.

"Mrs. Binton," the social worker said coldly, "you were supposed to be here yesterday."

"I am terribly sorry," Margaret said, "but I thought I explained. Thursdays are just impossible."

"Thursday is our clinic day for children under two. I don't see how we can get around that."

"How about," Margaret said casually, "thinking of Eric as a small two-and-a-half-year-old?"

Mrs. Regency's frown deepened and she bent down to take a closer look at Eric. The little boy smiled up at her.

"His nose is running," she said.

"Yes, they do that sometimes," Margaret answered. She

fished in her handbag, pulled out a Kleenex, and handed it to Mrs. Regency. The other woman awkwardly dabbed at the nose from a few feet away and tossed the tissue in a wastebasket nearby.

"Well, it's against policy, but let's see if they can work you in. I see he picked up a cold."

"Oh, the runny nose—that's probably from coming into such an overheated room."

"I find it comfortable," Mrs. Regency said and grabbed hold of Eric's stroller. "Better than too drafty. Follow me."

Eric was examined and proclaimed to be in perfect health, free of any signs of abuse, and three pounds heavier than when last seen. The nurse-practitioner was delighted with his progress. Mrs. Regency, perhaps still skeptical about his cold, offered nothing but a cautionary word about overfeeding on their way up to her office.

"I am sure you can understand," Mrs. Regency said with an empty and condescending little smile after they were seated, "we are very protective of our charges. They are in trouble when they get to us and we don't want to see it worsen. You'd be surprised at how often we have to change foster homes because the home-study worker made an error of judgment."

There was an awkward silence for a moment.

"For what sorts of reasons?" Margaret finally asked.

This time Mrs. Regency's little smile turned cold. "For whatever reasons we want," she said simply. She looked steadily at the older women by her desk. After another moment she continued. "Usually because we find the child and foster parent are not a good match. But you already know that, it's in our manual. Foster parents' rights are nonexistent until twelve months have passed."

It seemed to Margaret this last bit of news was delivered with a certain relish. She lit up a cigarette and sat back. Eric was busy trying to dissect a stuffed elephant on the floor.

"Yes, I understand that," Margaret said. "But that must be fairly uncommon. Certainly it's not good for the children moving them from one home to another. What they need more than anything is stability."

"In most cases," Mrs. Regency said and opened Eric's file on her desk. "Now let's see. He's had his inoculations, his monthly physical, there's no visitation . . . so as far as I can tell, the only thing we need to do in a few weeks is another home study."

"Another one?"

"Yes. To see how he's doing in his new environment."

Margaret crushed her cigarette out in an ashtray. "Well, any day is good except Thursdays," she said. "As you know."

Mrs. Regency looked at her calendar and penciled in a date two weeks in advance. Then she wrote it on a little card and handed it to Margaret. "There," she said. "I think that's all. Oh, wait . . ." she pulled out another pad and wrote something else. "Here is a voucher which you can present to Mrs. Edmonton. She's on the first floor, office number A-thirty-four. There shouldn't be too long a wait now."

Margaret took the paper. "For . . . ?"

"Reimbursement for carfare. Two dollars." Mrs. Regency stood up and glanced down at Eric. "He's certainly an attractive little baby."

"Aren't they all," Margaret said and lifted Eric back into the stroller. "One more thing. Do you have any idea how long it will take to come to some decision on Eric through the courts?"

Mrs. Regency turned her eyes slowly to Margaret.

"I have no idea," she said simply.

"I mean, where is his case? Is anything scheduled?"

"Mrs. Binton," the other woman said. "I don't see as how that concerns you. You are giving Eric a temporary shelter. While we attempt to make it as easy on our foster parents as possible, we do not include them in the legal aspects of a case."

"That is indeed shortsighted," Margaret said shaking her head.

"It is our policy."

Margaret held Mrs. Regency's eyes for a moment longer, then turned and pushed the stroller through the door.

"See you in two weeks," Mrs. Regency called after her. Then she sat back at her desk and made a note on Eric's file: "hostile foster parent." It had to be documented just right.

Eleven

THE QUEEN'S HUNTSMAN SNUCK UP BEhind little Snow White and lifted his sword over his head. As he started to bring it down in the murderous commission he had been given, almost every child and grown-up in the theater sank down lower in the movie seat, threw up a hand, or screamed to ward off the blow. The six old-timers sitting in the tenth row were no exception. But not Eric. He was too wrapped up in the swirling colors and motion of the Disney classic to be concerned with plot. Margaret, however, inadvertently threw one hand over the little boy's eyes, and grabbed onto Berdie's with the other. Next to her, Rena did the same with Pancher's arm. The moment passed, the huntsman spared Snow White, and a collective sigh went up in the theater. Sid, sitting next to Margaret, leaned over and whispered nervously in her ear, "You think this is all right for little children?"

"Rated G, isn't it?" she whispered back. "Besides, Eric loves it." The little boy had moved Margaret's hand from in front of his face and was leaning forward on her lap. He looked as if he wanted to dive into the screen.

There were perhaps forty people in the theater for the two o'clock screening. *Snow White and the Seven Dwarfs* had been in revival for over six months so many of the people were there for their second or third time. Not Margaret and her five friends. In fact Berdie, Durso, Pancher, and Rena had never seen it, while Sid and Margaret had seen it so long ago they couldn't come up with the name of even one dwarf. When they left the theater with big grins on their faces an hour later they could repeat the names of all seven.

"I can't remember when I had such a good time," Rena said to Berdie. "Didn't you just hate that evil queen? Reminded me of Frieda, the check-out girl at Sloan's."

"I liked Doc the best," Durso said. "He had the most developed collectivist spirit."

Sid gave the retired schoolteacher a playful nudge on the shoulder. "Old Walt would turn over in his grave if he heard that pinko claptrap." He turned back to Margaret. "Need help with the stroller?"

But Margaret had Eric buckled in his seat and was negotiating the open exit doors without a problem.

"It was a wonderful idea you had, Margaret," Berdie said. "I mean bringing us all down here. I would never have thought of it on my own."

"My idea," Margaret corrected her, "was to bring Eric. It was Sid's idea to join me." She looked at her five friends standing around on the sidewalk. "I suppose he should take the credit for expanding this into a matinee benefit. But," she smiled at them, "Eric and I certainly enjoyed the company."

"Wouldn't have missed it for the world," Sid said. "A classic like that." He bent down and repositioned the scarf around Eric's neck, then gave the boy's cheek a little rub with his knuckle.

"Still and all," Pancher said. "You'll have some explaining to do down at the OTB. You haven't missed the first race at Aqueduct in the last five years."

"Seven," Sid replied but waved it away. "Hell," he added, "I can miss a race now and then." He looked at Margaret. "Where you guys going now?"

Margaret looked at her watch. "I suppose I have time to do some shopping. We're running out of milk and diapers."

"You want us to take care of Eric while you go to Sloan's? We could play with him in the park."

"What, all five of you?" Margaret chuckled. "No, that won't be necessary. Eric loves to shop. You should see his little hands grabbing for things along the aisles. I think it's the high point of his week."

"Then how about some company in the store?" Rena asked shyly.

Margaret looked at all of them again. "What is this? A

month ago I couldn't get you to even think of helping, and now I can't keep you away. I don't understand."

There was an embarrassed silence for a moment. Finally Berdie pointed. "It's Eric," she said haltingly.

"What she means," Durso helped, "is that none of us knew what it would be like before. I guess little Eric has won our hearts."

"I am delighted," Margaret said. "But at this point, it's something like overkill. One person to help, perhaps two, but five . . . to take Eric to a movie . . ."

"Would've been six," Rena said sheepishly, "but I told Rose the wrong theater. I hope she's not still waiting."

"Rose?" Margaret said not believing her ears. "Take off the afternoon scavenging to go to a movie? Now that is something. Well, you can't all come to Sloan's," Margaret said, changing the subject. "And it's a little cold for the park. Why don't we go to the center? You can play with Eric while I shop. I don't think he'd mind missing just one shopping experience . . . after all, he's got the five of you to keep him busy."

"More like the other way around," Durso said with a grin and followed the little group as it swung uptown.

Margaret got the idea a week later. It came after seven days of being at the center of an ad hoc play group composed of eight senior citizens and one toddler. Besides this inner circle, at any one time a few of the other older people would come to have their coffee and watch the strange goings-on in the basement. A small collection of toys had mysteriously appeared one afternoon (rumored to have come from Rose, who had changed her scavenging route to include at least four Upper West Side nursery schools). Besides the toys, Rena got one of the local delicatessens to donate a dozen empty gallon cole-slaw and potato-salad containers, which made wonderful cylinders for building. Durso, not to be outdone, solicited and received a large reinforced cardboard box that previously had been the shipping crate of a twenty cubic foot, self-defrosting, automatic Kelvinator refrigerator-freezer. Durso, Sid, Roosa, and Pancher had wrestled it the five blocks to the center, where it had been converted into a little play house complete with a front door and two shuttered windows. Berdie and Alice had already painted out the big This Side Up and Use No Hooks lettering with a border of flowers and shrubbery. Next to the front door they cut in a little mail slot over which they carefully painted Eric's House.

Looking upon this scene—the toys, the towers of empty cole-slaw containers, the colorful play house, the seven other disheveled but involved senior citizens, it was no wonder the idea came to Margaret with the force of a revelation.

"What we should do," Margaret announced, "is set up a little nursery in our basement—not just for Eric, but for a whole bunch of these boarder babies. We have the space, we have the time, and it's obvious we have the energy and interest."

"What about the exercise room?" Berdie asked. All eyes at once went to Alice, who was just putting the finishing touches on a geranium she was painting in the left-hand window box of the cardboard house. She stopped with her brush in midair and looked back at them.

"This is a hell of a lot more fun," she said, "and probably more exercise, too. It's fine with me."

"Of course, we must ask the board of directors," Margaret continued, "but if we lobby a little from all our friends, maybe we can put enough pressure on them. This place is just too nice for only one child."

Everyone looked down at little Eric, who was trying to balance a fifth cole-slaw container on top of four others. "Besides, he could use some playmates his own age," Margaret said. She looked at the others in the basement. "What do you think?"

"The city would never allow it," Sid said. "To use the hospitals like a hotel service, take the kids out in the morning, bring them back at night. It'd never work."

"It might if we did it on a one-to-one basis. If each one of you were responsible for one child. Sort of like a big brother or big sister. Then, if we got some publicity and put some pressure on them . . ." She straightened out Eric's tower. "I can't imagine any official would rather see those children in cages than in a nice play area, with caring senior citizens watching them and preparing their lunches. Instead of a half a dozen foster parents and homes getting approved, all we'd need is approval for this one play center, and it's already a city-sponsored facility to begin with."

There was silence for a moment as the others glanced nervously at each other.

"Just look at what little Eric has already done for you," Margaret continued. "Three weeks ago you were a bunch of dried-up old geezers, filling empty days with makeshift activities; lounging on benches, drinking cheap wine, feeding pigeons, haunting OTB parlors. Here's your opportunity to do something really worthwhile. Think of it. Isn't a baby's life more important than who wins the fifth race at some racetrack in New Jersey for God's sake?"

Sid studied his shoes closely, then the pattern of the linoleum square he was standing on. No one spoke.

"Now look at you. You've come alive all of a sudden. And it's not just Eric, bless his adorable little heart. Any baby would have done the same, black, Chinese, Korean, Hispanic. Fortunately, one of the benefits of getting older is realizing that appearances are less important. Taking care of a child is a blessing all of us are capable of bestowing."

As a way of punctuating Margaret's little speech, Eric kicked the bottom container out from underneath, tumbling the others with a clatter to the four corners of the room.

"Margaret's right," Durso said. "The idea has merit. It's a kind of grass-roots socialism."

"'The idea has merit.'" Berdie repeated sarcastically. "Good Lord, can't you ever say anything with enthusiasm, like it's a goddamn great idea." She looked at Margaret. "It is, you know, and as far as I'm concerned, you can count me in."

"Me too," Rena said slowly.

"That's the spirit," Margaret said. "All it takes is a few and others will follow. Now all we have to do is convince the directors."

"How about a name for the nursery?" Sid said. "It's always good to give people something concrete to deal with, something they'll remember."

"Sid's right," Margaret said looking around, but no one had any immediate ideas. "Well," she said finally, "why not just call it the B and K Nursery?"

"B and K?" Rena said.

Margaret grinned, "For Biddies and Kiddies, what else?"

Twelve

ONE OF THE MOST HEAVILY GUARDED courts in New York City was at 60 Lafayette Street. Before gaining access to the elevator banks in the large, black Family Court building, one had to pass no fewer than four policemen and walk through an electronic detection device similar to those used in airports. Then, upstairs in the waiting rooms that formed the central hubs to the various hearing rooms, additional court officers kept watch over the people whose cases were about to be called. The city had not erred in placing so much manpower into "the black rock," as it was affectionately called, rather than into a precinct in East Harlem or Bedford Stuyvesant. Family Court was simply one of the most violent places in the city. Guns were constantly turning up in the machine downstairs, along with hundreds of assorted knives, and usually a good day for the court officers meant having to break up less than two fights before the lunch adjournment.

This was to be expected since Family Court brought together opposite sides in battles for the custody of children. If emotions ran high, it was because the stakes were astronomical. Parents lost their children, siblings were separated, families were reconstituted, and lives were wrenched into different orbits as summarily as the sound of a casebook closing on another disposition. The backlog was staggering and the steady flow of expectant faces into the courtrooms and the pained and angry expressions on the way out was inexorable.

But not everyone called into the hearings was a party to the case. Every parent came with a host of lawyers, social agency workers, case workers, translators, character witnesses, and in some instances, prison guards. The children, if they appeared, had only their legal aid lawyer in their corner. Presiding over this mass of troubadours brought together for a one-act play that seemed never to end was a judge expected to render a Solomonlike decision. The truth behind the black-robed officiousness was that deals were made even before the doors of the hearing room ever opened. Opposing lawyers agreed how to dispose of a case and then presented their recommendations. The outcome was about as much in doubt as the '44 presidential election. The judge cracked the whip, but it was over a team already pulling in one direction with skin as thick as boilerplate. Sometimes, in all of this, it worked. Most often the system merely perpetuated bad compromises and debilitating holding operations. It was no wonder there were so many guards.

Three weeks after Margaret's suggestion to her friends, Mrs. Regency found herself sitting on one of the benches outside hearing room number 27A. In her hand was the dossier on Eric Williams. She was not alone in her interest in the case. Seated alongside her was the attorney for the Youth Benevolent Association as well as the chief attorney for the SSC, Special Services for Children. They were all smiles, having cooked up a scenario for little Eric that everyone felt would be to his benefit. Eric was to be made a ward of the state, a designation that would then allow the adoption process to begin in earnest. The only fly in the ointment was the legal aid attorney, who was late and hadn't yet agreed to her client's disposition. Today was her intake day, in which she was so impossibly overloaded she hardly had time for her ten o'clock coffee. When she arrived she was over an hour late but quite unconcerned. She knew the judge probably wouldn't call the case until after twelve anyway.

The young woman sat down heavily next to Jason Sawyer, the YBA lawyer, and smiled wanly. She looked like she had just come from a Joni Mitchell concert, her long madras skirt and black turtleneck sweater concealed a short, somewhat overweight body. The inexpensive silver and bead earrings were too long for her face but were covered anyway by a hairstyle that looked makeshift at best. This was one lawyer who did not dress for success.

"Okay, let's have it," she said. "What are you recommending?"

"Termination of parental rights, ward of the state," Sawyer said. "Then Helen is going to start the adoption process. He'll be easy to place."

Sonja Miller, the legal aid lawyer, flipped through the five different files in her battered briefcase and picked out the one marked E. Williams. She opened it and spent three minutes leafing through its contents. The other two lawyers and Helen Regency waited politely until she had finished.

"Oh, yeah, this one," she said finally. "Parental rights on the father never existed so termination is unnecessary. The mother's death gives discretion to the court. But . . ." she added and went searching for another paper in the thick folder, "There's a relative I'm trying to follow up."

"What!" Jason Sawyer exploded. "What relative? There's no indication of any relative." He opened up his very expensive top-grain monogrammed leather briefcase and started looking through his own papers.

"It's unclear, a cousin, possibly a second cousin. One of my field workers heard about him last week and is trying to track him down."

"That's such bullshit," Mrs. Regency said. "You had months to uncover a relative and you only find him now. Where the hell was he when the SSC made their investigation?" She looked over towards the SSC lawyer, who just shrugged.

"Perhaps their investigators overlooked him because his last name was different," Sonja Miller said with a certain relish. "I wouldn't exactly say their people are in a league with P. Magnum."

"I don't believe this," Jason Sawyer continued and rolled his eyes. "A goddamn second cousin. What the hell good is that?"

"Why wasn't I told?" the SSC lawyer piped up.

"I'm telling you now," Sonja said. "And will also tell Judge Weill."

Helen Regency looked as if she might throw her file at the younger woman. "We're all set for disposition. Don't tell me you're going to ask for a postponement," she said angrily.

"Until I can clear up this loose end," the legal aid lawyer

said simply, "I owe it to my client to try and keep him with his family."

"That's a joke," Sawyer said and ran a hand through his slightly graying hair. "What rock did you find this family member under anyway? Weill will never give custody to such a tenuous relative."

"Perhaps not, but to continue your metaphor," Sonja Miller said with a smile, "we leave no stone unturned in our efforts. I'm asking Weill for two weeks. I'll have an answer by then."

"Christ!" Helen Regency said with resignation and snapped the file shut. "Bleeding hearts."

"Hey, we're supposed to be on the same side of the fence on this, for little Eric Williams's benefit, remember?" Sonja looked carefully at Mrs. Regency. "Meanwhile, how's he doing in his foster home?"

"He's with some old lady. Last time I saw them he had a cold. That's why I wanted the disposition."

"I'll visit," Sonja said. "And see for myself. It's only two weeks."

"He could have pneumonia by then."

"Better to have pneumonia with a family member," Sonja joked, "than be healthy with some stranger." She looked quickly at her watch. "Damn, I've got to be down in Part Two." She got up and walked over to a court guard nearby. She said something briefly to him, then passed back on her way to the elevators. "Don't look so glum," she said to Sawyer. "You'll win one tomorrow." She grinned and walked out, leaving them looking like the three bears before they spotted Goldilocks.

Thirteen

HAD THEY PROCEEDED THROUGH THE normal channels it would have taken Margaret's friends at least four weeks to pass through the foster parent review process. They found a shortcut, convincing the director of Metropolitan Hospital that the daily outings they planned would not only help the children, but also free up his short-handed staff for other important duties. He didn't need too much prodding since he had never liked the idea of using the hospital's staff for day-care duties. The best part was that it didn't cost him a penny.

The same week Eric Williams's case was postponed, Rena, Berdie, and Alice, along with two other women from the center who had become interested, were each given permission to care for a toddler between the hours of ten and four. A day after their approval, the little group went over to the makeshift nursery at Metropolitan Hospital and picked up their babies. Of the five, three were black and two were Hispanic. Along with Eric, six children were now making the basement of the Florence E. Bliss Center their daytime clubhouse. The trustees had not been easily swayed, but finally agreed to a trial period of a month to see if the arrangement disturbed the other, mandated functions of the center. Fortunately, the building had been built before the invention of Sheetrock. The pinochle and canasta games continued undisturbed by the muffled noise, except, of course, for frequent adjournments to go downstairs to see the kiddies. Most of the people who used the center were delighted that the basement was being put to such good use. It was inevitable that a few old-timers grumbled about the intrusion of the infants, but they were in a definite minority. In fact, in the weeks following the arrival of the Biddies and Kiddies Nursery, the center experienced an increase in its traffic. People were coming in who never showed up before except for the free Thanksgiving and Christmas dinners. They came, spent some minutes looking bored in the card room, then trooped downstairs to watch the children. They offered to rock crying babies, change diapers, and feed them their bottles; they offered to build blocks, race cars, and even play "horsie" on the mat with them. They did it because, in some magical way, the Florence E. Bliss Center had transformed the six individual children into a collective responsibility.

And they came bringing more donations. Outgrown clothes from grandchildren, strollers and prams from neighbors, toys from their churches and synagogues. And food . . . tons of food. Margaret and the others had to keep reminding many of them that one-year-olds could not handle things with nuts or pits like rugelach and Greek salad. But she was constantly amazed at the things they could and did eat, like little James, Berdie's black eleven-month-old, who could never get enough kasha varnishkes or Rosita, Alice's Puerto Rican charge, who just loved fettuccini, Alfredo or otherwise. Within a week of the children's arrival, the nursery in the basement was in full gear.

Sonja Miller arrived the second Tuesday of its operation at precisely three o'clock. The arrangements had been made the night before during her unexpected phone call to Margaret.

"You're his what?" Margaret had said when Sonja had introduced herself.

"His lawyer," she had repeated. "I represent him."

"His own lawyer?" Margaret was impressed. "Did I do something wrong?"

Sonja had laughed. "No, Mrs. Binton. But I've actually never seen my client. I'd like to meet you both."

"How much is he paying you?" Margaret asked wryly.

"Not enough for a cab ride. But the subways go uptown. How about tomorrow?"

So Sonja arrived for the first time that week on schedule and was shown down into the basement. The confused look was still on her face when she found Margaret playing patty-cake with Eric with the noise of five other toddlers surrounding them.

"An old-age home?" Sonja said.

"Not a home," Margaret corrected. "A center. There's a big distinction." She held her hand out. "You must be the shamus."

Sonja smiled and shook her hand. "And is this my client?"

"It is indeed. Stand up, Eric, and say a few words to Ms. Miller. Don't worry, it's all privileged information. Tell her what you had for lunch today."

"He can talk?" Sonja asked stooping to his level.

"Ten words. His most accomplished are 'habeus corpus.'"

"Good Lord," Sonja Miller said. "A foster parent with a sense of humor."

Margaret nodded. "I would say it's an occupational necessity. So, how can I help you?"

"I just wanted to say hello, Mrs. Binton, and answer any questions you might have."

"And check for cigarette burns?"

"No, that's not my job. I'm really on your side."

"You're kidding . . . ?"

"Well, really on Eric's. You come along with the territory." She looked around. "This is really quite nice. I don't think I've ever heard of this nursery."

"You wouldn't have. A week ago it was the Alice McIlvaney Sports Complex."

"Oh?"

"I'll explain some other time. I do have a question," Margaret said. "What's going to happen to Eric?"

"One never knows with these judges, but most likely he'll be deemed adoptable soon and YBA will find a permanent placement for him. I'm still following up something with his family, but I honestly don't think it is going to pan out."

"I see," Margaret said with a note of sadness. "And how long will that take?"

Sonja looked at her carefully. "Not long, maybe another week."

Margaret put her arms around the little boy. He looked up at her with a quizzical expression. A little tear formed at the corner of her eye.

"I know it's difficult," Sonja continued. "It's always hard on the foster parents."

"One would think," Margaret said without looking up, "that it's even harder on the children."

Fourteen

THE CITY ROOM OF THE NEWSPAPER where Peter Ryker worked was modern, brightly lit, and quiet, so quiet in fact Margaret thought she had walked into the accounting department by mistake. It didn't at all follow her notion of city rooms the way she remembered them from Howard Hawks's *His Girl Friday*, or *The Front Page*. Gone was the noise of reporters shouting for copy boys to run their stories down to composing, gone was the incessant *click click* of thousands of metal keys striking paper, the scores of bells signaling the end of typed lines, or the thump of a carriage return. The only thing that moved now were the hundreds of cursors that danced across the VDT screens, bathing the writers' concentrated faces in an eerie green glow. This was electronic city, where the only evidence of human intervention was found in the half-empty coffee cups. She picked Eric up out of his stroller and started threading her way through the orderly aisles of desks toward the back. Halfway across, she spotted Ryker staring gloomily at an empty screen.

"Well, well," he said when she came up. "What have we here? A future Pulitzer winner checking out the competition?" He bent over and gave Eric a friendly chuck under the chin. Then he got up, gave Margaret a hug, and dragged over a nearby chair.

"They said you'd be here writing." Margaret began. "Sorry if I'm intruding."

"That was optimistic of them. I'm here anyway."

"How's the leg?" Margaret asked.

"It's doing its job. I threw the cane away last week."

"Great." Margaret took a little Matchbox racer out of her pocket and gave it to Eric. For the moment he was quite content to sit on the floor and pretend he was Mario Andretti on a Le Mans circuit that included the chair and desk legs.

"Decided to take me up on the little tour of the paper, did you?" Ryker asked. "Perfect timing. I can't seem to work up any interest in this story about head lice in New York's private schools."

"I wouldn't think," Margaret said, "it was exactly your kind of reporting. Staten Island . . . ?"

"In the courts, which translates to 'deader than a doornail.' Come on, I'll show you around."

Margaret motioned him back into his seat. "I didn't come for a tour. I need some advice."

"From a reporter or a friend?"

"Both. I figure if you don't know the answers, you could find out." She flashed him one of her winningest smiles and sat back in the swivel chair. "What do you know about the laws governing foster care?"

Ryker looked at her closely. Then he glanced down at Eric doing figure eights around the linoleum squares. "I take it this is not totally unrelated to our friend here."

"Correct." Margaret fished in her handbag and retrieved her crumpled pack of Camels. In a moment she had one working and slumped back into her chair. "They plan to move Eric shortly. I know, Peter, I'm only supposed to be temporary, but I've gotten to love him and I'd hate to see him go to the wrong people."

"How do you know they'd be wrong? Could be they'd find him a young family, maybe with other children, and he'd fit right in."

"Maybe," Margaret said reluctantly. "Then again, maybe they'd find him a family that just looked good on paper and was really awful. His caseworker has no sense of anything, least of all who would be good for Eric. I just can't give him up without being sure of where he was going. Can you understand what I mean?"

Ryker looked down at Eric again and nodded. "I suppose I can. How long's it been now?"

"Six weeks."

"That's more time than I spent with Janet before I asked her to get married." He let that sink in for a minute and then continued. "So what is it you want to know?"

"I want you to find out what the regulations are, whether I have any say-so in regard to his eventual parents, or even how long I can delay things. I'm turning to you because I can't turn to anyone in the system."

Ryker grinned. "Give me a few days. I have a friend who could help and Janet might know something also. She's started looking into adopting through the city, although she's hoping my ski accident might have jarred something potent loose." He gave her a sheepish grin and leaned forward, "Now, how about that tour?"

"I think," Margaret said, looking at the retreating form of Eric driving his Matchbox car down the aisle of the busy city room, "it's already begun."

Fifteen

VICTOR LAZARRE WALKED INTO THE DeBeers head office at 17 Charterhouse Street in London with a certain stiffness. He was wearing his Saville Row chalk-stripe blue suit, his Turnbull and Asser hand-needled shirt, and his Sulka tie, but as far as he was concerned, he felt like he had just emerged from a sewer. The night before he and Susan had gambled at the Somerset Sporting Club until three in the morning, during which time he had consumed what must have amounted to a fifth of Scotch. The liquor was free, but the gambling had cost him several thousand pounds and all he had to show for it was a head as thick as curdled milk. He waited impatiently on the octahedron-patterned marbled floor, glancing often through the octahedron cut-glass panels in the entry doors. Octahedrons, being the shape of most natural diamonds, were big design elements at DeBeers. Within two minutes his broker from J. Fanning appeared and the two of them were quickly cleared past the two guards into the inner sanctum, the sight rooms of DeBeers. It was May 28, and one of the ten yearly sights was about to begin.

"You look like you could use some coffee," the broker said when they entered the central carpeted chamber off which the several individual sight rooms were located. "Stay at the club late?"

"Several thousand pounds late," Lazarre said. "Yeah, get me some black coffee. I can't do this if I'm seeing double." He slumped into a couch and watched as the broker went off in search of a DeBeers official. He looked around at the modern art and at some of the other dealers moving around. He nodded a greeting to Pierre Lacroix, one of the biggest merchants in Paris, and also to Henry Lunas, a friendly rival from New York. Then there were all those lousy Indians scurrying around like ants with their minions of counters. Lazarre had only one box to go through with perhaps one hundred to a hundred and fifty stones, each over two carats. The Indians, specialists in the small-sieve melée sights, had to work through dozens of boxes with pounds of tiny crystals. *Hell of a way to make a living*, Lazarre thought, and watched as his broker came back with the cup of coffee.

"Your box is ready," he said after setting the cup down. "Everything is in order. I checked them this morning."

Lazarre took a sip of the hot coffee. "But only one stone over ten carats, I noticed. I think you're pushing the good stuff over to Lunas."

"You can't have it both ways, Victor," the other man said. "This sight you've got over five hundred carats. Henry has considerably less."

"How much less?"

The other man smiled. "That, you know Victor, is privileged information. You should be delighted you're so high up on the list. Remember, you started with fifty carats. There are a thousand dealers who would kill to be sitting here now."

"Perhaps some already have," he said with a wink and finished the last of the coffee.

"Call me if you need me," the broker said and stood up.

Lazarre watched him head into one of the other rooms, then sighed, stood up himself, and walked stiffly over to his room. He opened the door, took off his jacket, and sat down in the blue upholstered seat at the work table to inspect his diamonds.

Even after fifteen years, this was always a time of stress for him. The stones were his, there was no getting around that. It was just a matter of seeing what DeBeers had done to him this time. Sometimes the colors were off grade and he'd have a difficult time placing the cut material. Sometimes the sizes were small and less valuable, or awkwardly shaped. But then again there were times he'd been pleasantly surprised and the material was large, choice, and very profitable. There was no telling until he actually sat down, opened the little brown cardboard container the size of a shoebox, and started working through the scores of diamond papers, each with its own surprise. The electronic scale was right by his elbow in case he wanted to check a weight, but more than that he had to rely on his eyes and his sense of what each rough stone could become. It was exacting work, made much more difficult by his throbbing headache. He was on only the twentieth stone when the phone in the room rang and took his attention away.

"Yes."

"Victor, the most wonderful thing . . ."

"Goddamn it, Susan. I told you never to ring me when I'm in a sight."

"I've got to talk to you, right now. I just got a call from home. Mrs. Regency had called."

"Who?"

"Helen Regency, from the Youth Benevolent Association. They have a baby for us."

"I don't give a damn what they have, I'm looking at close to a million dollars worth of diamonds here. It's gotta wait."

There was an intake of breath on the other end of the line and then silence. "It can't wait, Victor. I called her back. We have to be there tomorrow morning."

"Impossible."

"It's not impossible. Tell DeBeers to stick their stones in a safe for a few days."

"I can't do that."

Susan started crying. "It's a boy, Victor. His name is Eric. They had the hearing yesterday and he's now adoptable."

"Get a hold of yourself, Susan. It can wait."

"I've been waiting four years," she screamed into the phone. "Something might happen if we delay. Don't you understand, he's an adoptable little white baby boy." She took a breath and let that sink in for a while. "He's more valuable than your diamonds, Victor. He's more valuable than the goddamn Koh-i-noor." There was another pause. "I booked us on the Pan Am flight this afternoon at four."

"Are you crazy?" Lazarre said. "I won't be finished here before five o'clock. This is a DeBeers sight."

"I'm not getting through to you," she said. "Maybe this will. If I don't see you here in an hour, you can kiss your marriage good-bye. And with it, your house in Scarsdale and one of the Mercedes and a hell of a lot of money—more than what you're looking at right now!'' She hung up with such force that it made Lazarre rub his aching temple. He looked down at the cardboard box of diamonds and shook his head slowly.

''Women,'' he said angrily. ''The only worthwhile thing they ever do is buy diamonds.''

Sixteen

HARRY THE DOORMAN RAISED HIS EYES casually as Margaret Binton pushed into the lobby of the apartment building. She had the little boy by the hand and was pulling a shopping cart half filled with groceries.

"This came for you this morning," Harry said and produced a brown envelope with all sorts of markings on it. "Registered letter. I had to sign for it."

Margaret took it from him and looked at it curiously. When she saw the return address, her eyes narrowed.

"Bad news?" Harry asked.

"From these people, it couldn't be good."

She put the envelope in a pocket of her coat, took hold of Eric again, and continued on to the elevator. All the way into her apartment the unopened envelope seemed like a diseased thing, radiating evil. She felt a terrible urge to throw it down the incinerator shaft and be done with it. Once inside, she placed a toy schoolbus with all its knobby plastic children on the floor for Eric, made herself a cup of tea, and sat back to stare at the envelope. Finally she summoned up enough courage to open it.

> You are kindly requested to bring your foster child, Eric Williams, into the offices of the Youth Benevolent Association on Monday, May Twenty-ninth, at one P.M. for removal to his future adoptive parents' custody. Please bring with him all the clothing, toys, and paraphernalia that accompanied him to your foster home as your duties in regard to his maintenance will be terminated. We thank you for the

excellent and responsible care you showed during the period he was living with you. We hope you will volunteer again to take in another child.

The letter was signed, "Sincerely yours, Helen Regency."

Margaret nearly spilled half of the tea, her hand was shaking so badly. Her eyes teared over for a moment when she reread the word *terminated*. It was coming, she knew, but this was a nasty way to treat someone who had been taking care of and loving a child for about two months. Her sadness turned to anger when she realized that this was nothing more than a personally typed form letter, a cold kiss-off without so much as a note of understanding of the foster parent's loss. If this was how they treated people, God help little Eric.

She picked up the phone and dialed the number penciled nearby. After the connection was made she spoke quite clearly.

"Mr. Peter Ryker," she said. "In the city room."

"You have ten days," he said after she told him about the letter. "I found that out this morning. I got a friend up in Albany to grab me a copy of the New York State Department of Social Services regulations. They can't take him away unless his safety is in danger before that. In that time you can file for a conference to ask why they are removing him. They have to see you within another ten days. Then they notify you of their decision in writing and then they have to wait another three days before they can grab him. Hell, they can give you a date all right, but you can fight right back."

"So, what's that?" Margaret said. "Twenty-three days maybe?"

"About. But wait, there's more. Section 400 of the Social Services Law. If you don't like the decision to remove the child after your conference with the YBA people, the law permits you to have what they call 'a fair hearing' with a referee assigned by the State Department of Social Services. They have another thirty days to let you know of that decision. Now," Ryker took a deep breath, "if you don't like that decision, you can appeal the whole thing to family court. All the while Eric gets to stay with you. When you know the regs, it's not so easy for them to get their hands on our boy."

"Thank you, Peter. I was hoping there was a way to delay things."

"You want to hear something else? They should have notified you when he became adoptable. As a foster parent you have a right to know that. You don't have preference in any adoption until after he's been with you for twelve months . . ."

"Twelve months . . ."

"Right, but they're still supposed to let you know and also let you know the procedure of applying to adopt him . . . and of the provisions of the adoption subsidy program. Did they do that?"

"Are you kidding?"

"I didn't think so. You got a case, kiddo, a good case. There's enough here to throw a dozen monkey wrenches into their plans."

"Good, I'll get started right away."

Seventeen

MARGARET WROTE THE LETTER ON HER best stationery, the stuff with the monogram on it she'd gotten as one of Oscar's last gifts. Had he known she'd be using it shortly for condolence thank-you notes when he gave it to her? She had always wondered about that. It was a typically obtuse way for her late husband to let her know he was dying. Poor Oscar, a man so unlike her, unable to confront anything directly but who had second sight into things that were always surprising her. She thought she had put his death seven years earlier well into perspective, but he was really still there. She found herself writing the letter to the agency with the heaviest of hearts; on the one hand fighting for little Eric, on the other thinking of her husband. It wasn't true that the older you got the better you could deal with loss. The older you got the more ghosts you had inside and each new loss caused them to rise up and rattle their chains . . . for the most absurd reasons, for little blue monogrammed notepaper. She wiped away the moisture that had formed at the corner of her eye and sealed the envelope. *Now*, she thought, *let's see how they like that.*

The next day, Mrs. Regency walked into the office of Charles Wright, the director of the Youth Benevolent Association, with an expression on her face that could have cut steel. She dropped Margaret's note on his desk and gave him a moment to read the message.

"The nerve of her," she spluttered. "That's never happened before. And I have the Lazarres coming in at noon—from London."

Her supervisor looked up and pushed the note back across his desk. "Call Sawyer and see what he says."

Regency looked pained. "I did. He's going to research it but unfortunately he thinks she's within her rights."

"So, give her the ten days. What else can we do?"

"I told the Lazarres they'd have Eric this afternoon."

"I guess they'll have to wait," Mr. Wright said. He leaned back and Regency could see that the much-abused center button on his single sport coat had finally given up the good fight. It had been pulled off and now the jacket no longer held in check the mound of flesh beneath. Wright caught her looking at his ample torso and leaned forward.

"What about the conference she's asking for?" Regency continued. "We've got to give reasons why we're taking a young infant away from a seventy-two-year-old woman?" She sounded exasperated. "She says she's going to have representation."

"So, let her have representation. There's every reason for moving that child to a younger, comfortable family that can give him a loving, stable home. We'll have our little conference, we'll listen politely to her objections, and the Lazarres will still get him. It's only ten days."

"They won't be happy," Mrs. Regency said. "The Lazarres are very . . . demanding people."

"They'll wait," the director said. "Set up the conference with the foster mother for June eighth and I'll come. Get Sawyer also. Now," he bent back to a report on his desk, "you'll excuse me, I have this funding request to read."

Regency turned and left the office, but she wasn't happy. The Lazarres wouldn't like it. They wouldn't like it at all.

Eighteen

TEN DAYS LATER, MARGARET'S REPRESENtation consisted of Peter Ryker. They sat on one side of the table across from Helen Regency, Charles Wright, Jason Sawyer, and a secretary who was recording the meeting. No one looked nervous at the start; that is, not until Ryker informed them of his affiliation with one of New York's dailies. After that disclosure, the atmosphere in the room changed. What was going to be a breezy nod to a foster parent's complaints turned into something more formal. Everything was done properly. They listened politely to Margaret's descriptions of Eric's particular needs, they listened to her reservations about letting Eric go into a family she had never met, and they listened to Margaret's concern that he would be emotionally affected if he was suddenly removed. In the end Sawyer agreed to review their order with Wright, told Margaret they would let her know their decision, then stuffed all the papers back in his briefcase and stood up. Everyone shook hands and left the hearing room.

"So, what did you think?" Margaret asked Ryker hopefully on the pavement outside.

"Time for the second letter," he said, "asking for the referee. Their decision was made before we stepped in the room. Polite, yes, but sympathetic . . ." Ryker shook his head. "Three days and you'll get their new removal order. Better be prepared."

Margaret sighed. "I'd still like to meet the adoptive parents."

"Maybe you will," Ryker said. "I think you got that point

across. After your next request, don't be surprised if they come to visit."

"I certainly would have some questions to ask them," Margaret said. She took a few steps, then suddenly turned to the younger man. "Peter, am I being too fussy? After all, the agency's screened them. Presumably they're okay."

"Don't presume anything," Ryker said. "This is a city of eight million people and seven million incompetents." He smiled. "No, Margaret, I don't think you're being too fussy. We're talking about a little baby here."

The agency's two-page follow-up letter came a day later explaining why, after due consideration, it was still imperative for Eric to move immediately into an adoptive home. Once again they thanked Margaret for her concern, but offered her nothing of what she requested. Eric's removal date was now set for June 11.

Margaret wrote back demanding a fair hearing by a state Department of Social Services referee and notified Sonja Miller, Eric's legal aid lawyer. Sonja had been friendly enough the one time they had met at the center, and had even called later when the relative she was tracking down turned out to be a false lead. She appeared sympathetic and Margaret figured that at the very least she could make sure that the Youth Benevolent Association adhered to all the regulations. The legal aid lawyer agreed to follow up on the letter and attend the hearing whenever it was scheduled.

When the call came, Margaret, as politely as she could, informed Mrs. Regency that the date scheduled for the second meeting with the referee was impossible.

"No, I'm afraid I am unavailable next week."

"What!" Mrs. Regency exploded. "But it's all set."

"I guess it will have to be reset," Margaret answered. "Section 400 of the Social Services Code does not specify the fair hearing has to be done at the convenience of the agency. Normally one checks with both parties before any mutual appointment is made. In theory, Mrs. Regency, I am doing your agency a favor, something you lose sight of, and if you want to schedule a meeting then you had better check with me for when it's convenient."

"Well, I never . . ."

"And it's not convenient next week. It will have to be sometime later in June."

There was a silence on the phone while Margaret waited.

"The director will call," Mrs. Regency said finally in a voice so tight it was barely over a whisper.

"Well, I won't wait his call," Margaret said. "I'm taking Eric out to the park now. Oh, and Mrs. Regency," Margaret took a deep breath, "tell the director that at the hearing I intend to ask why, as your regulations require, I was not informed when Eric became adoptable. That and a few other questions I have."

Mrs. Regency slammed the phone down so hard it made Margaret wince. She turned to Eric and shook her head.

"My goodness, she was upset." She bent down to do up his jacket. "All I want to do is meet your new parents."

Nineteen

MARGARET LOVED THE FLOWERS MOST of all. Central Park had wonderful specimen trees, berry bushes, rock outcroppings, meadows, and lakes, but the flowers of June always won her heart. After years of walking through its paths, she knew where the tulips were the most varied, the iris the tallest, and the lilac the thickest. On that particular afternoon she treated Eric to a tour, taking him from the entrance on Eighty-fifth Street down to the sailboat pond and then back out on Seventy-second Street. As far as Eric was concerned, the flowers were okay, but the double-masted remote-controlled ketch that he spotted at the pond was something else. He watched for over fifteen minutes while it glided mysteriously back and forth across the glassy surface. Margaret stood the whole time, afraid to let go of his hand while they stood so near the water. When they finally arrived back at her apartment Margaret felt as if she was carrying around two watermelons for feet. On her way towards the elevator, Harry stopped her.

"Some people been here looking for you. Ain't none of your friends, though."

Margaret stopped and turned towards him. "Any message?"

Harry nodded. "Said they'd be back later. But hey," he winked, "you must be coming up in the world."

"Why's that Harry?"

"You should see the size of the rock on her finger. You could play football with it."

"Two people?"

"Yeah. With a guy that people usually open doors for."

"So," Margaret smiled, "how'd he get in?"

Harry laughed. "I guess he figured a way. He had this attitude about him, Margaret, you know, like he expected people to fall on their face or something."

"Said they'd be back?"

"S'what he said."

"Good, send them up next time. But buzz me first, I want to get Eric looking nice."

"So who is it?" Harry asked.

"His new parents." Margaret said and pushed the stroller on towards the elevator.

The intercom buzzed about an hour later, just when Margaret was getting Eric up from his nap. In two minutes he had on a clean shirt, new sneakers, and his hair was neatly brushed. With all that, the little boy was still rubbing his eyes on the couch when Margaret went to open the front door. Standing there were two very uncomfortable people. The woman was looking at the scratched and chipped doorframe suspiciously, as if it might be harboring some terrible bacteria, while the man was staring straight ahead, as if to pierce the door with the force of his vision. Margaret couldn't tell whose cologne was stronger, the Chanel No. 5 or the concoction he wore that smelled of musk and sandalwood. But Harry was right, the diamond was a real stunner. It kind of framed the dialogue to come. *You listen*, it said. *We'll do the talking*.

"Yes?" Margaret asked.

"Susan and Victor Lazarre," the man said. "Eric's new parents."

"Come in," Margaret offered and stood back. "But I think it's premature to refer to yourselves as his parents just yet. There's one more hearing to be held."

The woman gave her husband a steely glance and walked in. Her close inspection of the doorframe now extended to the interior of Margaret's apartment. From the look on her face, what she saw didn't please her any better. Then her eyes fell on the little boy and she gushed.

"Oh, darling, look, there he is. Our Eric." She glided over, picked him up, and gave him a hug. Given this treatment from someone he'd never seen, Eric squealed and squirmed so much that the woman had to drop him back on the couch. Margaret came over to comfort him.

"I guess he's not used to so much attention," the woman said pointedly.

"No, he's not used to you, that's all. Give him a moment." She put Eric on the floor with one of his toys and stood up. "Have a seat," she said. "Would you like some tea?"

"Nothing," Victor Lazarre said. "Just a few minutes of your time."

Margaret looked down at Eric nearby. "Perhaps you'd like to play with Eric for a little so he could get to know you better. He particularly likes his Matchbox cars."

"No, what I have to say is really for you." Lazarre dropped into Margaret's comfortable wing chair by the couch and pulled out a package of Dunhill cigarettes. "We got a telephone call today from Mrs. Regency. You know who she is."

Margaret nodded. "Indeed."

He pulled out a cigarette, tapped it on the box, then lit it. "She recommended that we come and see you. She is convinced you are doing everything to abort Eric's adoption because of personal, selfish, and irrational reasons."

"Is she?" Margaret said, feeling her blood rising. "Do you mind?" She reached a hand out before he could pocket the cigarettes. He opened it and let her take one out.

"She thought that after meeting us you might be persuaded to take a different attitude."

"Mr. Lazarre," Margaret began. "My reasons would appear irrational only to someone who has no feeling for children, like Mrs. Regency. Eric has been my son for some time now, and I am not willing to pass him over to just anyone. He is not a football."

The woman's eyes narrowed and she took a step closer.

"We are not just anyone," she said. "My husband is Victor Lazarre, one of the most important people in the diamond industry."

"That may well be," Margaret said. "But it appears he has no interest in playing with and getting to know this little boy. That tells me more than any *Dun and Bradstreet* report." She lit the Dunhill and leaned back in the couch. "Besides, it's not irrational to want to know where he is going."

"Where he is going," the man said, turning a light shade of red, "is into a home where he will never need for anything. Into a home where he will get the best education New York has to offer, the chance to travel and see the world, a secure, wonderful future."

"Sounds like an Army recruiting speech," Margaret said. "What about love?"

"Of course love," the woman said in a rising voice. "We wouldn't be here if we didn't think we could love a child."

"One doesn't have to think about those things," Margaret added softly.

Susan Lazarre threw up her hands. "Victor, talk to her," she said. "You know . . ." she left the sentence unfinished.

"You can only delay so long," he added. "We have the system on our side, not to mention a team of private lawyers ready to initiate any action I tell them to."

"That sounds like a threat, Mr. Lazarre."

He looked at her closely. "Take it any way you want. Eric is going to be our child, with your agreement or without."

"Because if it is a threat, I want to be sure I understand it correctly."

"Victor!!" the woman said.

He looked over at his wife and frowned, then he turned back to Margaret. "Susan is right. There is no need to get heavy-handed here." He took another puff of his cigarette and crushed it out. The anger drained out of his face and a new smug look crept in. Margaret noted the change.

"I only mentioned the lawyers as a last resort," he continued. "Certainly that can be avoided."

"Yes?" Margaret took another puff of the Dunhill and looked over at Eric. She felt a slow sadness take hold of her. Here were his appointed new parents, so well versed in threats, posturing, and materialism, and so little endowed with sincerity and affection. They were absolutely the wrong people for her Eric.

"I noticed, for instance, that your apartment could use some new furniture . . ."

Oh God, Margaret thought.

"And maybe a new paint job. It must have been several years since the last one."

Margaret just looked at him, not moving.

"New York is an expensive city. Now, my wife and I are willing to, um . . . give you a contribution to make losing Eric a little easier to bear. You can look at it also as a token of our appreciation at how well you took care of him while he was here." Lazarre smiled and reached into his breast pocket. His hand emerged with a clean white unsealed envelope in which Margaret could see a neat stack of bills. "Three thousand should do it," he said and tossed the envelope on the coffee table between them.

Margaret felt a shiver run through her. She was speechless, looking down at the envelope like it was some dirty and scabrous thing. Finally she cleared her throat.

"Three thousand will not do it—Eric is not for sale," she said. "Take your money and get out." She looked up at them, first the man, then the woman. Then she looked at Eric again and began crying.

No one moved for a moment, then Mrs. Lazarre snatched up the envelope and said, "You're just a stupid old lady."

"Get out!" Margaret shouted and stood up. She walked over the two steps to the child, picked him up and hugged him. He was not used to her raised voice and threw his arms around her neck for comfort.

"This is not the end of it," Victor Lazarre said, the anger once again behind his eyes. "Not the least of it." He stood up and turned towards the door. "Let's go," he said to his wife. "This place is depressing."

Margaret watched as they exited. Not once did they look at the child.

"All they had to do," Margaret said softly after they left, the tears still in her eyes, "was say you were wonderful and that they wanted to love you. That's all. I would have been satisfied."

Twenty

"THEY TRIED WHAT?" RYKER COULDN'T believe it.

"Three thousand dollars," Margaret said.

"Unbelievable. The stupidity . . ."

"That was after they threatened me with lawsuits. I suppose I should have guessed when I saw the Dunhills." She pulled back from the table as the waitress brought over her bacon cheeseburger. Eric, seated on a high chair at the end of the table at Starks, was treated to a French fry.

"Stupid," Ryker repeated. "You going to tell Regency?"

"Are you kidding? For all I know she suggested it."

"You're not just going to let it slide?"

Margaret shook her head slowly. "No." She lifted the cheeseburger and took a bite. She watched as Eric waved the French fry around like a baton, then stuck the whole thing, including two fingers, in his mouth.

"It's tricky but I suppose you could go to Regency's boss," he said.

"It's not enough. First of all, it's just my word against theirs, and I don't like the odds . . . two against one." Margaret took another bite and washed it down with a sip of cherry Coke. "Besides, it's no good just stalling now. I believe him when he said the system is on their side . . . and the connections, and the money. I have to gamble and maybe get to the root of things."

"Meaning?"

She looked closely at Ryker. "Meaning it's possible I'm

not the first person they threw money at to get Eric. And if that's true, then there are other, more serious implications."

Ryker picked up on it right away. "You think Regency is on the take?"

"You're a reporter, Peter. Think about what constitutes a good lead. Motive and position." She put the sandwich down on her plate. "Look at her. She controls dozens of adoptions a year. One word from her and family Smith gets baby Jones . . . or maybe they don't. And when there's a particularly marketable baby—and don't kid yourself, babies are commodities—think how tempting it would be to put the bite on people like the Lazarres. She's already got their economic profile from their application papers. It would be so easy for her to pick out a few couples a year to deal with and no one would be any the wiser. Lazarre offered me three thousand to avoid a few weeks' delay. Think how much he'd pay to get the initial nod."

Eric reached over to Margaret's plate for another French fry but was handed a morsel of meat instead. "We can't forget your protein now, can we," Margaret said. "He loves hamburgers. There's no hope he'll ever be a vegetarian." They both watched as Eric worked his jaws over the chopped meat until it was the consistency of purée.

"It could be a little dangerous finding out," Ryker said, returning to the previous discussion.

"Listen, Peter, even if I convince them the Lazarres are wrong, Regency will find someone else equally as bad. Besides, Lazarre's only threatened me so far with lawyers."

"It's my experience," Ryker offered, "that when you uncover someone's scam they usually turn nasty, that's all. It's also my experience that those kinds of under-the-table transactions are untraceable. There's usually no loose ends around. No correspondence, deposit slips, stuff like that. Mostly everything in cash."

"So," Margaret shrugged, "we have to tackle it from the other end. We have to find someone who paid Regency money."

"The Lazarres?"

"They'd be too wary. No, someone in the past, someone who thinks that it's all over and done with."

"Don't ever underestimate the power of gab," Margaret winked. "Especially with a grandmother. What I need, though, are the names of past YBA adoptive parents."

Ryker took a breath. "That won't be easy."

"I think I've got an idea," Margaret said. "And in case it doesn't work, I want to find out more about Victor Lazarre. Maybe we can even the odds somewhat." She looked at Ryker. "That's where you can help. Maybe there's something in his past that he forgot to put on his adoption application."

"Like what?"

"I don't know. You're the investigative reporter, not me."

Ryker exhaled. "I'll see what I can do. I have a friend at the paper who has contacts on Forty-seventh Street."

"One more thing," Margaret said slowly. "Do you think you could get me a little tape recorder from the paper? Something that's not difficult to operate and would fit nicely into a handbag?"

Ryker shook his head slowly but there was a smile on his face. "Margaret, I don't know about you."

"I'll need it in a few days."

Eric slammed his fist on the table and made the cutlery jump. Margaret grabbed for her throat.

"Goodness, I'll never get used to the noise. I think he's telling us it's time to go."

"You'll be careful?" Ryker asked.

"I'm seventy-two," she answered. "Isn't that proof enough?"

Twenty-one

"HELLO, IS THIS THE YOUTH BENEVOLENT Association?" Margaret said into the telephone. "Yes, I'd like to speak to your person in charge of custodial services."

"I guess that'll be Mrs. Woodruff," the receptionist said. "Hang on."

Margaret looked up from the telephone at Alice standing by the desk. They had gotten permission to use the phone at the Florence Bliss Center while the children were downstairs playing in the nursery. Alice had an expression on her face that made it clear she had no idea what was going on.

"Mrs. Woodruff here."

"Oh, Mrs. Woodruff," Margaret began. "How do you do. My name is Florence Barnes, the purchasing agent for Quality Electronics Incorporated. I was given your organization as a reference."

"Yes?" Woodruff said slowly. "For what?"

"We are having trouble with our current custodial service, and I am seeking bids for the next year's contract. We are dealing here with some very sensitive parts, I needn't tell you, so I only want to include companies with good references. Now I understand you're quite pleased with your service. At least that's what the people over at Custom Custodial Care said." Margaret looked up again at Alice and waited.

"I'm afraid there's some mistake," Woodruff said. "We don't use anybody by that name."

"Wait . . ." Margaret made a sound of rifling through some papers on the desk that happened to be a two-day-old copy of the *National Enquirer*. "A Mr. James of Custom Custodial said they've been sending people to your West Forty-ninth Street location for the past several years. Said you were very happy with them."

"Absolutely not. Mrs. Barnes, you are being mislead."

"Oh, that's funny," Margaret said. "Perhaps they use a different name. I think he said they have a few different units."

"I've never heard of a Mr. James or Custom Custodial," Woodruff said definitely. "But if you're seeking other companies, why not try Unified Maintenance, that's who we use."

Margaret winked at Alice. "And you're pleased with them."

"Yes. They do all right. It's mostly cleaning the offices. We get our own people to straighten up the places where the kids play."

"Thank you," Margaret said. "They're in Manhattan?"

"Yes. I can give you the number."

Margaret listened, wrote something down, thanked her once again, and hung up.

"Now," she said standing up. "Alice, you're about my height. Let's see if we can get you a job at Unified Maintenance for a day or two."

"What kind of a job?" Alice said with extreme skepticism.

"Oh, just a little cleaning and dusting. They'd never take me, I'm too old. But as I recall you're only sixty-three."

"Where am I going to clean?" She asked with a frown.

"I could care less," Margaret smiled. "I only want the uniform." She looked at Alice more closely. "On second thought, when they outfit you, get something a little baggy. All that exercise has done you some good."

Three nights later, at precisely 6:30 P.M., Margaret was waiting on the street in front of the Youth Benevolent Association office. For the past two hours she had been sitting in Ryker's car a few steps away, watching while all the workers had left. Mrs. Regency came out at precisely 4:30; Charles Wright, the director, left an hour later. By 6:30 the traffic coming out of the building had slowed to a trickle and Margaret figured it was about time to wait on the street. She patted Ryker on the knee. "Come back for me in a couple of hours," she said. "Rose is sitting for me and I promised her I'd relieve her by nine."

She didn't have long to wait. In five minutes she noticed a middle-aged black woman trudging towards her a half block away. The brown and tan uniform she wore was exactly like the one Margaret was wearing, right down to the U.M. Inc. insignia on the pocket. She waited until she was a few steps away before giving her a cheery greeting.

"Hi," Margaret said. "You from Unified Maintenance?"

The other woman looked at her and nodded slowly.

"Who are you?"

"My name's Sarah," she said. "Sarah Rompkins. You must be . . ."

"Angelina. What 'cha doing here?"

"They didn't tell you over at the office?" Margaret looked flustered. "I'm just starting so they wanted to break me in with someone who knew the ropes."

Angelina gave her a close inspection, including her uniform, then a little smile lit up her face. " 'Bout time I got some help. How they figure this is a one-woman operation I don't know. You ever work this kind of job?"

"In a hospital," Margaret said, bending the truth a bit.

"Then you know it's not a layback job. We just do the offices here, but we still got to hit the floors."

"I'm good with a scrub brush," Margaret said.

"Not me," Angelina said. "Only thing I like to do on my knees is pray. Let's go. We got several hours ahead of us."

Margaret followed her up the front stairs and into the building. There was still a guard on the door, but he was too interested in his Watchman TV to do anything more than nod them in and lock the door behind them.

"We go up to three," the black cleaning woman said.

"Don't worry," Margaret said. "I'm right behind you."

Two hours later they made it up to the fourth floor, where both Helen Regency and Charles Wright had their offices. Margaret's back was beginning to bother her and her fingers were aching and raw from all the water and disinfectant. She had been following Angelina around emptying trash baskets, mopping and scrubbing floors, and straightening up desks. Angelina assured her that the fourth floor, with fewer offices, should go quicker. She unlocked all the doors on the corridor and headed for the end office.

"You coming?" she asked Margaret.

"Listen, why don't I start here and work my way down. Then when I meet you we'll be done."

Angelina thought this one over and shrugged. "Okay, but don't make a mess of it. I'll get the blame."

Margaret turned into the first office and flipped on the light. *Woodruff's office*, she thought, *nothing here*. She did a fast clean and went on to the next one, which was Regency's. She left the door slightly ajar and set to work quickly.

She checked the desk first but found only current files of cases Regency was handling mixed in among three or four paperbacks with titles like *Desdemona's Desire* and *Castle of Dreams*. The top-drawer tray held stubs of pencils, paper clips, leaky Bic pens, and in the back part, petty cash slips, as well as a bunch of bills from the Eighth Avenue Health and Aerobics Club. Margaret closed the drawer and moved over to the small gray filing cabinet, the logical place for any records to be kept. She pulled on both drawers with equal results. The damn thing was locked. Then she thought about the pencil tray in the desk again and went back to look underneath it. No key, only some stubs held together by a paperclip. Looking closer she noticed they were pawn tickets from someplace called Lucky's Pawn Shop up in Harlem.

"How you doing, honey?" she heard from Angelina down the corridor. "Need any help?"

"Fine, just fine," Margaret called out, copying down the details of the tickets. When she had finished she turned quickly to look over the room. *Now where in God's name would I keep the key if I were her?* Her eyes scanned the desk top but there were no boxes or places to hide it, only a Rolodex, some magazines, a glass ashtray, and a fluorescent lamp . . . unless—Margaret didn't believe Regency could be that obvious—unless she put it here . . . She flipped the cards in the Rolodex to K, and reached inside.

"Have you found it yet, honey?" Angelina called.

Margaret stopped dead still, her hand inside the Rolodex, her fingers just touching the thin piece of metal filed under K.

"Found what?" she shouted back, her voice shaky.

"Salvation, child. Christ Jesus." Margaret pulled her hand back with the key as Angelina came in through the door. "Times like this at night when I get so lonely I seek the Lord. He's always with me, you know."

"Is that so?" Margaret said, feeling like a kid caught with her hand in the candy jar. "You've been saved then?"

"When I was eight."

"It must give you great comfort," Margaret said, itching now to get at the cabinet.

"Like a rock." Angelina took a step closer. "You should try Jesus. 'The Lord knoweth them that are his. And let every one that nameth the name of Christ depart from iniquity.'" Angelina smiled benevolently. "Second Timothy, chapter two, verse nineteen."

"I'm afraid it's a little too late for me," Margaret said.

"Jesus said, 'For every one that asketh receiveth; and he that seeketh findeth; and to him that knocketh it shall be opened.' Matthew, chapter seven, verse eight."

"Well maybe," Margaret said. "But Jesus is not going to help us do the floors now, is he?"

Angelina gave Margaret a hard look, then shook her head sadly. Without another word she headed back into the other office and a minute later, started humming a gospel tune.

In no time Margaret had the two drawers of the cabinet open. There were all sorts of files, too many for her to go through individually. Most were marked with old case numbers and had disposition sheets stapled to the front. One or two were marked "Adopted," but did not indicate by whom or where to look for a reference. Perhaps, she thought, all records of adoptions were really sealed and her task was hopeless. She reached in deeper. In the back she came up with a file titled "Parent Services," and then with another marked "Prospective Adoptive Families." This second file had the applications of over fifty families who were seeking children. There were no comments by Regency on the applications except that several of them had little red checks after their names. Were these the ones who could best pay her fee? Even if that were true, it could never be proven. Idly she leafed through the second file. She passed over sets of lists such as "Foster Parent Briefing Sessions," "Abused Children Counseling Service," and "Vocational Seminars,'' until her eyes landed on one called ''Adoptive Parents Discussion Group.'' It was simply a list of people who were involved in a bimonthly rap group to talk out some of the difficulties of being adoptive parents. There was no identification of the children involved, either by sex, age, race, or date of adoption, but still it was something. Margaret copied the names down as quickly as she could. When she was finished she put everything back in place, locked the filing cabinet, and replaced the key under K.

Coincidental with her closing the Rolodex file, Angelina walked in the office again. She took one look around and frowned.

''What's this?'' She asked. ''Doesn't look like you've done anything. Cigarettes in the ashtray, papers in the garbage . . .''

''It's my back,'' Margaret said and winced. ''I had to take a break.''

''Lord, the help they give me,'' Angelina moaned and shook her head. ''Pray to Jesus, honey, he'll help your ailing back.''

''I think a hot bath would probably do just as well. I'll be all right in a few minutes.''

''In a few minutes I want to be on the A train heading uptown. Here, let's knock this room off and call it a night.''

The two women worked for another fifteen minutes and then turned off all the lights on both floors. They left the building and on the pavement outside, Angelina turned to Margaret with a look of concern on her face.

''I didn't want to say nothing, but you know, honey, ain't you getting on a little for this kind of work?''

''I am,'' Margaret admitted. ''I think I bit off more than I could chew.''

''Hell, honey, you bit off enough to gag on. If I was you, I'd try something less strenuous, you know, like something in sales.''

''There's an idea,'' Margaret said and held her hand out. ''Thanks, Angelina. It was a pleasure working with you.''

They shook hands and then parted, Angelina heading for the subway and Margaret toward the corner, where Ryker had returned.

"You get anything?" he asked after she eased herself into the passenger seat.

"I think so," she said. "Either a pulled sciatica or a herniated disc. Let's go, Rose and Eric are waiting."

"That's all for over three hours' work?"

Margaret grinned. "Some curious pawn tickets and a bunch of names . . . oh, yes, and a suggestion."

"How's that?"

"Sales. The woman I worked with thought I should go in for sales."

Ryker laughed. "You must have misheard her."

Margaret frowned.

"I think she meant safes." He slipped into gear and shot out onto Tenth Avenue. "I think we found you a new career."

"You ever hear of a place called Lucky's Pawn Shop up on Saint Nicholas Avenue?"

"Who hasn't?" Ryker said. "Up in Harlem, Lucky's is the black equivalent of Morgan Stanley."

"Then we might have something," Margaret said. "At least it's worth a visit."

"I think I just got elected," Ryker said.

"I think so."

Twenty-two

THE NAME OF THE ESTABLISHMENT OBVIously had nothing to do with the nature of the clientele. When Ryker walked into Lucky's Pawn Shop the next morning, the five people on line looked like they were hocking their last earthly treasures. One showed a ring with a purplish stone that would have been at home inside a box of Cracker Jacks. Another had a wristwatch that was probably telling time while Nixon was telling the nation about his dog Checkers. The man ahead of Ryker had a clarinet that was so worn its ebony finish looked gray under the overhead fluorescents.

Ryker took in the space around him with the eye of a practiced reporter. The man sitting on a stool by the corner reading a boxing magazine was probably Lucky's security system. Nothing sophisticated, just a two-hundred-and-sixty-pound mean-ass, pistol-packing, high school dropout pulling down a hundred and a half a week to scare the daylights out of any would-be robber. He looked like he would truly enjoy throwing somebody through the plate-glass window if he was told to. Around the side walls of the store were counters with the unclaimed merchandise. But Lucky's main business commodity was currency, not merchandise, except maybe the knives in a little case by the window; knives to skewer a chicken, cut a watermelon, or carve a rival gang member. They were the only hot item at Lucky's, that and the money, which constantly trickled out from under the payout window in front.

The clerk behind the window had a jaded look that said he'd seen it all; junkies trying to sell stolen merchandise, children trying to sell their parents' jewelry, boyfriends hocking mink coats while their owners were out working. If you lived in Harlem, you made a pilgrimage to Lucky's at some point. There were other pawn shops, some more convenient than all the way over on Saint Nicholas Avenue, but Lucky's had one thing going for it—they never asked questions. You had the merchandise, they had the money. And when the police came to look at some of the items, Lucky, whose real name was Damon Haynes, invited them into the back for a chat. A half hour later they would leave with maybe two or three repossesed items and smiles on their faces bright enough to light up the Apollo Theater. Lucky understood the equation early on; pawn brokers who asked too many questions wound up sweeping their own floors. Ryker figured that if Regency was orchestrating some kind of scam, Mr. Haynes, in all probability, was first violin.

The man in front stepped away from the window with his twenty dollars and it was Ryker's turn. He moved closer to the glass separating him from the clerk.

"Lucky in?"

The other man inspected him carefully, "Maybe," he said, "but if you're hocking something, you're talking to the right man." He motioned behind him to the gold-testing kit, the electronic scales, the loupes and magnifying glasses, and of course the calculators and cash register. "Lucky doesn't change my appraisals."

Ryker nodded. "I didn't think he did, but I want to make a deposit, not a withdrawal."

The clerk held his gaze for another few seconds, then stepped back from the window. He motioned Ryker to another glass partition, then spoke a few words into an intercom and turned back to his place by the front.

A minute later a tall man in an Italian-cut gray silk suit emerged from a recessed door and stood in front of him. Once again Ryker was inspected, this time by a pair of eyes that went about their business with a surgical precision. They looked at his face, his designer jogging outfit, and his Reebok sneakers and after another few seconds Lucky Haynes leaned forward and said, "Well, you ain't a cop. What you want?"

Ryker looked over to the clerk, who was now inspecting a used 35 millimeter camera. The kid who was offering it looked young enough to be in grammar school. "We go inside?" Ryker asked. "This place is like Pennsylvania Station."

"That depends," Lucky said. "What the subject matter is."

"Ten thousand dollars."

Lucky didn't hesitate. A broad grin crossed his face and he leaned forward to press a button. A door in the partition a few steps away buzzed and swung inward. "Ten grand," Lucky said, "entitles you to a seat. Follow me."

Lucky's office looked nothing like his store. The metal door between them separated two spaces as dissimilar as the employees' pantry and the Grand Ballroom at the Waldorf. A gray plush carpet covered the floor, a chrome and smoked glass desk faced into the room from one wall, and modern art, lots of it, covered the walls. Lucky had built himself nothing less than a multinational corporate office, but on ground level, yards away from the decaying trash-filled lots of Harlem. All that was missing was an English-accented private secretary.

"I don't know you," Lucky began as he eased himself into his black leather Eames desk chair. "Should I?"

"No," Ryker said simply. "But this city is full of people like me. Too much cash and no place to lay it down quietly."

"What makes you think you could leave it here?" Lucky wedged a manicured nail of his thumb between his two front teeth and watched Ryker's reaction.

"I think we have a friend in common. Nicky Bates."

"You know Nicky?" Haynes asked, raising an eyebrow.

"Yeah, just casually. But before he went upstate he told me about you. You can ask him."

"That's dumb. How you think I'm gonna ask him up in Attica?"

"Come on, Lucky, way I hear it, you wanted to have a bachelor party with hookers in the prison snack bar you could arrange it."

Lucky looked at him silently for a moment, then leaned back in the chair. "Maybe I could, and maybe I couldn't. Besides, a lot of people know Bates. What'd you say your name was?"

"Ryder, Peter Ryder."

"You know, Ryder, I could just say I have no idea what you're talking about and leave it at that."

"You could, but then you'd miss out on a profitable little

deal. Bates told me, but I forgot. What commission do you take?"

Lucky narrowed his eyes, but didn't say anything. He was still working his fingernail in the space between his teeth, still trying to get a handle on this man he'd never seen before. Any bro with ten grand in cash in Harlem was someone he certainly should know about. "You got the cash with you?"

Ryker smiled. "Depends on the terms. If it's too expensive I might just buy me a thick mattress."

Lucky laughed. "There's no mattress thick enough the feds can't cut through. Besides, ten thousand in small bills can get pretty lumpy. It's not worth the insomnia." He laughed again, this time at his own joke. "'Course you could always bury it somewhere, but who wants to have to remember half a dozen holes all over the city—or, for that matter, pay their tailor with moldy bills. Terms . . ." Lucky leaned forward with a look like he had come to some decision. "I'll tell you the terms." He checked them off on his fingers. "Absolute safety. No one thinks of robbing Lucky because my system of criminal justice works a lot quicker than Koch's. We're open six days a week, ten A.M. to twelve midnight, so if you want a couple grand at eleven P.M. you got it. Try that at a cash machine." Lucky continued. "Hot coffee in the mornings and hot telephone numbers at night. What more you want?"

"The house vigorish," Ryker said.

"Twenty percent. Up front."

"Twenty . . ."

"That's right. Dirt cheap. If it was hot money and you had to go overseas to launder it, it'd cost you up to fifty."

"What if it's cold as ice?"

"Then go to Citibank with it. What you bothering me for?" Lucky looked at Ryker now with some suspicion. "We got a deal or what?"

"Twenty percent," Ryker repeated.

"For total secrecy. You make a withdrawal, I check it off here. You can keep your own record on a scrap of paper if you want and I'll initial that too. It's a sweet deal, Ryder, a service I've been providing since Nicky Bates was still pushing reefer on a Hundred and Twenty-fifth Street. Take it or leave it."

Ryker looked at him steadily, then nodded once. ''Sounds okay to me.'' He stood up and took a step towards the door.

''Hey, where you going?''

''You see any pockets in this jogging outfit? I'll be right back.''

Lucky Haynes narrowed his eyes. ''You do that, bro. I'll be waiting.''

''Twenty minutes,'' Ryker said and reached for the door-knob. ''Just a quick round trip to my Sealy Posturepedic.''

''Just make sure,'' Lucky said, ''you don't take a nap along the way.''

Twenty-three

MARGARET LEANED BACK IN THE COMfortable couch and lifted her feet up. The bridge her legs made was just high enough for the three-year-old to crawl under.

"Active, isn't he?" Margaret said.

"Wait, it's only ten-thirty. He's not even warmed up." The little boy's mother bent over and straightened up his collar, then leaned back in the couch next to her visitor. "He takes a nap at three, but the rest of the day it's just go, go, go. Makes me wonder what I spent all my time on before Jason arrived."

"Still," Margaret smiled and lowered her legs again, "they're such a joy to have around. That's why I came to see you," Margaret added.

"Yes, you already explained," the other woman said. "But I don't think I can help you. I sympathize with your daughter and her husband, but there's really no easy way. It took us about six months to get Jason but that's because we didn't specify a race, or a sex, or anything in particular. If they want a little white baby . . ." she shrugged, "it could take years."

"That's what they're finding, but I thought people who have been through the process might have some insight into, you know, shortcuts."

"Patience," the woman said. "That's all." She looked down at her son, part black, part Hispanic, but in any case one hundred percent toddler. "We gave up on that route long ago."

"Well, my children are trying to make one more stab at it," Margaret said. "That's why I got the bright idea of seeing if there was a discussion group of adoptive parents in the city. I mean, you're all success stories, all adoptive parents. There's got to be some trade secrets among your discussion group."

"Possibly, but keep in mind none of us went the private lawyer route. Most of the children are nonwhite and some are handicapped."

"But not all?" Margaret said casually.

The other woman hesitated. "No, not all. There are two white babies in the group."

Margaret bent down and scooted a wooden locomotive towards the little boy across the linoleum floor. The child smiled delightedly, turned, and scooted it back. "And who would they be?" she asked.

"The Barnetts and the Stafford-Parks. Roger and Amanda are the children. I'm sure the parents won't mind your asking. The worst thing we all figured is to hide the fact that our children are adopted."

"Mmm," Margaret said and volleyed the locomotive back. "Well, you've been very helpful. I have no idea if this will do any good, but after all the pain that Harriet and David have been through, I just thought I had to try something myself. Call me an old meddling grandmother, if you like, but there it is." She stood up and shook the other woman's hand. "Jason is a wonderful child. I wish you all the luck in the world."

"Just give me four more hours sleep a day and I'll be happy."

"Ha," Margaret said as she headed for the door. "Just settle for a hot cup of tea when you can. Sleep . . ." Margaret shook her head, "is for old people like me." She waved good-bye and was gone.

The half-hour interview with Mrs. Barnett proved to be thirty minutes of wasted effort. Roger was napping when Margaret rang the bell, so his mother was only too delighted to sit and chat. After all, Margaret came with the greetings of Jason and his mom. But Mrs. Barnett had no inclination to discuss Roger's adoption particulars. All she would admit to was that she had waited a long time for him and was surprised and delighted when she got the call from Mrs. Regency. Margaret, in very delicate ways, kept prodding around the issue, but Mrs. Barnett was unyielding. Several times during their chat Margaret fingered the buttons on the tape recorder in her handbag, but she kept the machine playing just in case. But nothing surfaced, just compliments about the YBA and their handling of the adoption process. When Roger's scream alerted his mother that his short, peaceful nap was over, Margaret politely excused herself.

That left the Stafford-Parks, with an address on east Ninety-fourth Street between Lexington and Third. Twenty minutes later Margaret found herself ringing the front doorbell of a small private town house with window boxes full of geraniums. After a considerable wait, she rang a second time. A few moments later the door opened and Margaret found herself facing a woman in her late sixties with an open, curious face. The apron she was wearing was smeared with the same brownish substance that was on her hands.

"I'm sorry to trouble you, but I'm looking for Mrs. Stafford-Park," Margaret said. "Is she at home?"

"I'm afraid not, dear, she's out of town. Perhaps I can help you."

"You are the cook?" Margaret asked slowly.

"No," the other woman said and laughed heartily. "I'm the mother-in-law, baby-sitter, and currently gingerbread baker. My granddaughter specified cupcakes for her nursery-school birthday."

"Gingerbread cupcakes?" Margaret said in some dismay.

"That's what she wants. With banana frosting. Now why is it, do you think, that everyone is so sure grandmas know how to bake? I feel as out of my element as Tallulah Bankhead in *Lifeboat*."

Margaret laughed. "At least you don't have Walter Slezak as a neighbor." She moved up a step. "You know, gingerbread is my favorite. Perhaps if you let me help you with the cupcakes, I won't have to trouble Mrs. Stafford-Park when she returns. It was really Amanda I wanted to talk about."

The woman in the apron looked carefully at Margaret, at her gray hair neatly coiled in a bun, at her oversized handbag, and at her very sensible shoes, and took a step back.

"How about the banana frosting?" she asked.

"That too," Margaret said, and walked the rest of the way up the steps. "Now, first of all, I'll need another apron."

The kitchen was a masterpiece of urban renovation, from its granite countertops and marble floor to its Portuguese tile splashboards and high-tech digital equipment. Its cost, figured back on a per-meal basis, probably brought the price of dinner at the Stafford-Parks up to the level of a modest entrée and dessert at Lutèce. And it was all a mess. Cake flour was over the countertops, eggshells were underfoot, and there were enough dirty bowls in the sink to have prepared an Indonesian *Rijstafel*. In the center of all this were two cupcake tins, still unbuttered and quite unfilled.

"And the batter?" Margaret asked.

"I had to throw it out. It tasted awful."

"Well then," Margaret said. "I guess we'd better start from scratch."

In twenty minutes everything had been cleaned up, and Margaret was just combining the molasses and honey with the grated orange rind in preparation to mix in with the baking soda, cinnamon, and ginger. When it was just the right consistency, she began stirring the flour in a little at a time.

"I should have just bought the packaged stuff," the other woman confessed. "But her mother doesn't like all the chemicals they put in those mixes. Next time I'll let her make them."

Margaret put the tins in the oven and began on the frosting. "Will she be back for Amanda's birthday?"

"Yes, they'll be back tomorrow night. They took a quick week's vacation in the islands."

"Good, then they'll be able to taste your handiwork."

"Yours, you mean. I don't know how to thank you."

Margaret smiled. "After the frosting, let's make a nice cup of tea and have a chat. There may be a way."

They hunkered down at the kitchen table, still in their aprons. The gingerbread was starting to fill the kitchen with its sweet earthy aroma mixing now with the pleasant smell of freshly crushed bananas. In front of each woman was a cup of tea. Margaret reached into her handbag, fumbled for a moment, then pulled out a cigarette. The other woman looked longingly at it, so Margaret reached back in and got another one for her.

"Mind you, I'd never buy a pack," Amanda's grandmother said, "but it's certainly a pleasure when I can filch one. My son doesn't like to see me smoking."

Margaret nodded and held out the match to her new friend. "Now, Constance, there is something I'd like to ask you."

"Yes, about Amanda. You said so on the front stoop."

Margaret inhaled deeply, crossed her fingers under the table, then chose her words carefully.

"I should start by telling you that Harriet, she's my daughter, is a lawyer and her husband, David, is in television. With one thing and another they kind of postponed their family plans until they got their careers set. These days I guess that's understandable, but it didn't make me any less impatient to be a grandmother. I kept asking them how about it and they kept politely telling me to mind my own business. Well, I suppose you know how it is." She took a puff of her cigarette and looked at the other woman who was listening carefully. "Of course when they finally got around to it it was too late—something about Harriet's tubes that wasn't right."

"Mmmm, with my son it was a low sperm count," the other woman said and took a sip of tea.

"I can't tell you what a blow that was. Of course they got a few other opinions, but unlike the joke, changing doctors didn't work. I wanted to yell at them, 'see, I told you so,' but that wouldn't have helped. They were in so much pain, but it was only the beginning." Margaret pulled a handkerchief out of her sleeve and began worrying it between her hands. "So they thought of adoption, which opened up a can of worms you wouldn't believe. Lawyers, ads in little hick papers, unlisted numbers. It was getting so that Harriet, she's a trial lawyer, was losing all of her cases, she was so upset. Nothing seemed to work—so many false leads, trips to nowhere, heartbreak. For every baby in America, there are a dozen people after it." Margaret now daubed at her eyes.

"White babies," Constance said simply. "Mark and Marilyn went through the same thing."

"I couldn't just stand by and watch all that. I decided to see if there was some other way, maybe something they hadn't explored. A friend of mine works at the Youth Benevolent

Association, and she told me about your discussion group. I thought I might ask some of the parents how they went about finding their children."

"You mean Amanda?"

Margaret nodded and took a sip of tea. "Anything. I can't tell you how much it would mean to them . . . and of course, to me. Making gingerbread cupcakes is no fun unless you have someone to give them to."

The other woman put a hand on Margaret's arm. She squeezed it lightly. "I know. You spend all your life raising children and then when they've grown up, poof, it's over . . . and it's sort of like you're over. What's to look forward to, a dinner once a month, a couple of phone calls they wedge in when they remember? Without Amanda . . ." she shook her head, "I'd be lost."

"Your husband?" Margaret asked.

"Died a few years ago."

"Oscar too."

The two women sipped their tea in silence for a minute and looked at each other.

"You have to go to the right people," Constance said finally.

"Here in the city?"

The other woman nodded. "At the YBA. They don't get little white babies often, but when they do, you have to make sure you're first on their list."

"How do you do that?" Margaret asked innocently.

The other woman smiled softly, said nothing, but rubbed her thumb and forefinger together.

"Money?" Margaret said in a low voice. "You're kidding." She leaned closer. "How much?"

"Now, you didn't hear this from me," Constance said and upended her teacup.

"Of course not . . ."

"Thirty thousand—at least that's what it was two years ago."

Margaret put a hand to her chest and she wasn't acting. "Dollars or rupees?" she exclaimed.

Constance laughed and when she was finished, she lowered her voice a notch. "In cash, they were told, all very hush-

hush, of course. But look, it worked. Everyone's happy as can be."

"Thirty thousand . . ." Margaret repeated. "I had no idea."

"Yes, and more when they see they have you hooked. But we were lucky. Mrs. Regency named her price and stuck to it."

"Helen Regency," Margaret spoke clearly. "At the Youth Benevolent Association. She's the one you gave the thirty thousand to?"

The other woman hesitated just a second. "I don't know if I should be telling you this, but yes, and the next day Mark got a call from her telling him the paperwork was all finished and they could pick up Amanda that evening. Very efficient she was. That's what I mean. It's just a matter of knowing who to go to." She checked her watch and stood up suddenly. "I think the cupcakes are done."

"Oh yes," Margaret said and followed her to the oven. "I'll get the frosting ready." The two women bustled around the kitchen for another few minutes until the cupcakes were out of the tins and lined up on a plate and Margaret was hovering over them with the bowl of frosting.

"I'm sure Amanda will love these," her grandmother said. "It's just what she wanted."

"Well, one good turn deserves another," Margaret winked at her and applied some frosting. "Now if we can just get what Harriet and David want . . ."

"You will, I'm sure. Just be subtle about it."

Margaret smiled. "The heart of discretion, Constance, I guarantee, the absolute heart."

Twenty-four

"THANK YOU," THE WOMAN SPOKE SOFTly into the phone. "I'll wait." She drummed her finger on the tabletop as she heard the ubiquitous Muzak sliding down the line at her. Finally the receiver was picked up and a familiar voice got on.

"This is Judy Barnett," she said. "I thought you should know about something that just happened, something peculiar."

"What is it?"

"Somehow, a little old lady got hold of the list of the discussion group and came to visit me. She was on her way to the Stafford-Parks and had just come from some of the others. I thought you said that information was confidential."

"It is."

"Not if a seventy-year-old gray-haired lady with a Timex watch and runned stockings can get it, it isn't. And she started asking some very probing questions."

"Like what?" Mrs. Regency said.

"Like was there anything I could tell her how I was able to adopt Roger. She didn't actually say money, but I suspect that's what was on her mind."

Now there was a distinct pause on the phone, the only sound coming from a tapping, probably that of a pencil or pen at the edge of a desk. Finally Mrs. Regency said, "You didn't tell her anything, did you?"

"No, but who knows what the others said?"

"I see. Could you describe this lady? Did she, for example, smoke a lot?"

"Yes."

"Camels?"

Now it was Mrs. Barnett's turn to hesitate. "How'd you know?"

"Never mind. I think I know who it is. Don't worry, I'll take care of it."

"You'd better," Mrs. Judy Barnett said. "There weren't supposed to be any complications, ever. That's what you said."

"And there won't be. You won't hear from her again." The phone went dead in her hand. She turned and looked at Roger, but the feeling she had was not one of maternal pride. It was one of fear.

Twenty-five

THE FLOWERS WERE STILL THERE, AS WAS the sailboat pond, but today Margaret had another treat in store for Eric. Stratford-on-Avon it wasn't, but rowing a boat on the lake by Central Park's Bethesda Fountain was as close as you could get. Big granite outcroppings ran down into the tranquil water at the lake's north end, while gently sloping lawns and meandering walks bordered its southern end. On a day when the sun was shining and the temperature was over 70 degrees, the lake was dotted with scores of rowboats, some with lovers, some with parents and children, some just with individuals who wanted to take a break from city life for an hour. Out there in the middle of the lake, with the towering oaks and specimen pine trees insulating against much of the noise and blocking all but the very tops of the skyscrapers, one could actually imagine a Manhattan of simpler, more bucolic times. Birds came down to the shore to peck in the mud for edible slugs and worms, squirrels performed gymnastics in the bordering branches, and insects, even occasional butterflies, ventured out across the surface of the water. The lake was a joy to everyone who used it, and Margaret was determined to introduce Eric to its magic.

The best way was to rent a boat. But while Margaret had mastered other two-handed activities, like knitting, when it came to dipping two oars into the water at the same time and pulling evenly, she was hopeless. So she invited Sid along to provide the propulsion and also to help watch that Eric didn't tumble into the water. They walked to Seventy-ninth from her apartment, took the crosstown bus, then entered the park on

Fifth Avenue. Twenty minutes later they were at the Loeb rowboat concession and just fitting a life preserver over Eric's shoulders.

"Give us a dry boat," Sid said to the young man dispensing the little craft. "I can't tell you how many colds I've gotten through my feet."

Margaret shooed Sid ahead of her into the flat-bottomed boat and gently lifted the boy over to him. Eric was frightened at first by the rocking movement of the boat, but soon he spotted a duck in the water nearby and pointed at him.

"Duck, d-u-c-k," Margaret said. "Duck."

"Dut," he repeated, and they were off, pushed from behind by the concessionaire. Sid took the oars and started paddling. They had an hour, plenty of time to explore everywhere, so he took a leisurely pace. Bethesda Fountain slipped past on their left and they continued around to the other side of the lake. There were several other boats on the water, but it was easy enough to avoid them. Besides, the old rowboats were so thick that it would have taken an iceberg to stave one in.

Margaret held Eric close on her lap and started describing the points of interest. Besides the duck there was Mr. Squirrel, Mr. Fish, and Mr. Frog, Big Rock and Mr. Bridge. Mr. Bridge was Eric's favorite and he made them paddle underneath the high-humped wooden structure several times. Halfway through their hour Sid rested and they just drifted. Everyone was in a friendly mood. People in nearby boats waved, making sure they were not blocking their way, and one young woman even paddled over to give Eric a balloon. There was one more little cul-de-sac to explore before heading back and Sid unshipped the oars and rowed toward it. It was a protected little cove, perhaps forty yards across, lying in the shadow of one of the more northerly outcroppings of rock. It took them five minutes to get there and another five to skirt the shore. Margaret pointed to a small stream that was helping to fill the lake, and then Sid headed the little craft back in the direction of the boathouse across the lake.

"Be careful of that other boat," Margaret said to Sid, who had his back turned. She pointed toward another rowboat just rounding the outcropping and heading into the little cove. Sid glanced over his shoulder and made a correction with his left oar. He took two more strokes, then turned around again. He let the boat drift and just watched as the other rower continued toward them.

"Margaret . . ." Sid began.

"What is it?"

"I may be crazy," he continued, "but I think the man in that boat was in the crosstown bus with us. Something about his face . . ."

Margaret glanced past Sid's shoulder at the other boat but just shrugged. If he had been on the bus with them or not she couldn't remember. Perhaps she had been too preoccupied with Eric. But his face was one not easily forgotten. His eyes were so close together, she thought amusedly, that they both could look through the same keyhole together. And his haircut . . . she hadn't seen such a close crew cut since Haldeman had graced the television news. But what was truly remarkable was the man's chin. From a distance of twenty-five yards it looked like it took up almost half the man's face, the kind of chin a cartoonist would give some Nazi colonel in a World War II comic book. She motioned with her hand.

"You'd better move a little to your right."

Sid pulled again a few strokes on his left oar and the boat swung over. They were now about thirty yards from shore and about twenty yards from clearing the little cove. Except that with a few swift strokes, the man in the other boat angled his boat around and was now still heading in on them. They were only fifteen yards apart and closing.

"More right," Margaret called, this time with a rising voice. The last thing she wanted to do was test the strength of their boat's side planks. Instinctively she tightened her hold on Eric and waited for the two boats to change course to avoid each other. Sid swung right a few more degrees and would have passed if the other oarsman hadn't also changed his direction.

"Is he crazy?" Margaret shouted. "Watch out!" But it was too late. The heavy boats came together with a dull thud and glanced off each other harmlessly.

"You dumb jerk," Sid called out. "What do you think you're trying to do?"

The other man reached over and grabbed their bow painter

and held on. A playful little smile crossed his mouth but it didn't have any effect on his acre of chin.

"Hey, just a minute," Margaret called out.

"No, you wait just a minute," the other man said in a voice that sounded as if it had been washed in broken glass. "I got a message for you." With the hand not holding the rope he reached under his jacket and withdrew an ugly little gun made uglier by the stubby silencer on the front. He held it close so that it was hidden by his body. "You're getting too nosy about this kids stuff. It's none of your goddamn business, understand?"

Margaret looked quickly around but there was nobody nearby. The other boats were out on the main part of the lake, perhaps eighty yards away, and the shore was empty.

"So this here is just a little warning," the man continued. "Next time I won't be so friendly." Without changing his posture or moving anything more than his index finger, he pulled off three quick shots. The noise sounded like little harmless pops from holiday noisemakers, there was no force or menace in them. But the effect they had on their boat was a different thing. All three of the shots had passed through the floorboards between Margaret and Sid's feet and splintered out three separate holes the size of silver dollars. Immediately the brownish, mud-stained water of the lake began rushing into their boat. Both Margaret and Sid looked down in wonderment for a moment, then Margaret shouted, "Paddle, Sid, paddle!"

Sid took a few strokes but the other man was still holding the bow rope. Their boat stayed where it was. Without thinking, Sid pulled an oar out of the lock and raised it over his head to throw. The other man just pointed the gun casually at his heart and said calmly, "Sit down."

"The baby can't swim," Margaret yelled. "You want to kill an innocent child?"

The other man looked at them for another few moments, checked the level of water in their boat, which was now up to their ankles, and finally dropped the painter. He put the gun back and quickly began rowing out of the cove.

"Not that way," Margaret said urgently. "It's too far." She quickly scanned the edge of the cove looking for a spot they might climb out, but it was all steep rock. "Not here either."

"I think I remember a spot," Sid said, "just around the edge." He fumbled with the oar for a minute, then started pulling in the direction he had indicated. But the boat, heavy under normal circumstances, was now as sluggish as a barge full of sand. The water level was up to their calves and still rising. They had maybe three minutes before the gunwales went under.

"Can you bail?" he shouted.

"With what, my eyeglass case?"

Sid grunted with the effort of rowing. The boat was moving ahead but painfully slowly. Eric was jumping up and down on Margaret's lap with delight.

"Wa-wa, wa-wa," he kept saying.

"How deep is it here anyway?" Sid said puffing.

"Who knows? Can't you go any faster?"

"You want me to have a coronary?"

"I'm sorry." She peered over the edge but couldn't see beneath the muddy surface. For all she knew it could be twelve inches or twelve feet down. Good Lord, when was the last time she'd been swimming—Coney Island maybe, 1958?

The situation was becoming hopeless. They weren't making all that much headway toward the spot Sid had mentioned. Besides, the boat had its own momentum and changing directions once they rounded the outcropping would be almost impossible. Sid trailed the oars for a few seconds to catch his breath. At that moment the boat scraped the bottom. They were still ten yards out, still filling with water. The stern where Margaret was sitting got heavier and started tilting down under. She lifted Eric and started sloshing up to the bow.

"This is as far as we go," Sid said. "The rest of the way it's on foot."

Margaret looked at the shore, which was sheer rock, then down at her dress, soaked up to her knees, and her handbag, sodden with the dirty water, and shook her head.

"I'm not moving. What if we drop Eric?"

"He has a preserver."

"The rocks are too steep, I won't risk it. Someone will come." And as if by imperial decree, at that precise moment a voice hailed them over the water. A voice with a distinct accent.

"I say, are you having a bit of a problem?"

Margaret looked at the approaching rowboat with its two obvious tourists, and shook her head in disbelief.

"That's about the biggest understatement I've ever heard."

"Be thankful for the weak dollar," Sid said, and with careful aim, threw them their line.

Twenty-six

THE EIGHTY-SECOND PRECINCT ON MANhattan's Upper West Side was a curious amalgam of old and new. When it was built, the architect must have figured that ponderous stone portals, eight-foot oak doors, and sixteen-foot ceilings would intimidate the criminals of the city into respect for the law. They were, after all, only people-sized, the Irish heist artists, Italian extortionists, and Jewish confidence men, while the space for their initial encounter with Justice was truly Olympian. That was back in 1892. By 1988, when New York's criminals respected nothing short of speedy arraignments to get them back out on the streets, compromises had been made. The vaulted lobby had been double-decked to provide space for the community affairs unit, the intradepartmental liaison office, and a few small interview rooms. The space beneath, fronting on the duty sergeant's desk, was barely eight feet high and had lost a lot of its grandeur. The walls were an art gallery of off-color patches and peeling, eczema-like flakes, and the floors, stained a rusty brown at the base of the radiators, bore reminders of dozens of cracked fittings. That was the old part. The new part was the computer on the duty sergeant's desk, and the smile on his face. McSweeney, not one given to casual levity, had last smiled in public during the sixth game of the '86 World Series. But then he had had a twenty riding on the game with his brother-in-law from Boston.

"Margaret, my God it's good to see you," he said in an unabashed Irish accent. "Now where have you been?"

"Busy, McSweeney. Very busy. Is he in?"

McSweeney nodded toward the back. " 'Tis your lucky day,

my dear, he's in a passable good mood, too."

Margaret arched an eyebrow in a silent query.

"The new car he's been promised finally made an appearance," McSweeney said. "He won't be having to take clinkers anymore to crime scenes. Go on back. I'm sure he'll be delighted." He turned toward the computer screen and Margaret noted that once again he wore an expression that went with the decor—cold, solid, and very businesslike. In a minute he was talking to some slouching youth. Margaret slipped around the desk and knocked on Lieutenant Morley's office door.

"Yeah," a voice said. "Whadda ya want?"

This is friendly? Margaret wondered, and stepped into the office. Morley was by the window looking out at something in the parking lot next door. Even from the back, Margaret could tell he had been putting on weight. His shoulders were stretching the seam in his serviceable Bonds jacket until it looked ready to release his beefy torso like some overripe seed pod. He turned around reluctantly and Margaret could tell that the weight had not only gone to his body. If this kept up, come Christmas time they'd have their Santa Claus for the kids at the nursery.

But Morley had the kind of face that gave nothing away. Ideally suited to looking at a busted flush while bidding for the pot, it also did pretty well concealing his current state of mind. The lines in it, and there were enough for a man pushing fifty-five, all seemed noncommittal, neither smile or frown lines. In fact, most of his features were nothing out of the ordinary, no scars or broken cartilage, nothing bent or twisted. All was quite expected—except for his eyes. Except for the eyes he could have been a man selling silk ties behind a counter at Saks, or maybe a man driving an elevator in some Park Avenue co-op. The eyes, however, took all those options away. The eyes said, *Be careful, I'm way ahead of you, Jack.*

"Margaret, what the hell are you doing here?"

"My God, Sam, you never change. The epitome of hospitality."

"Cut the crap, Margaret. Have a seat. The only time you come to see me is if you need some help." He tore himself away from the window and the comforting view of his new car, and walked the few steps to his desk. He sank down into the swivel chair with a soft sigh.

"What's with the sneakers?" he asked. "You taking up jogging?"

She waved away the question. "I walked through a big puddle this morning and had to change shoes." She looked closely at him. "You know Sam, twenty pounds less and you'd be a lot happier."

"Don't I know it. You come in to discuss the state of my health or what?"

"Not really, but I've never met anyone who couldn't use a little mothering now and then. Probably all those starchy foods you eat . . ."

"What else?" Morley grumbled. "I don't have time for this now."

Margaret eased down into her favorite chair, the oak one by his desk and ashtray, and straightened a wisp of hair in front of her forehead.

"Quite simply," she began, "I need a tiny favor."

"That's what I thought. What sort of tiny favor? The last one I remember having to explain to the commissioner."

"I just need a little information on someone. I couldn't think of any better way of getting it than to go to my good friend Sam Morley."

"Oh, that kind of information," Morley said and shook his head. "You know that's way out of line. Giving out police records for private use."

"Come on, it's done all the time. Any private investigator worth his salt has contacts and ways of getting that kind of stuff. My luck, I happen to have a lieutenant as a friend." She gave her winningest smile.

"Your luck you have a lieutenant as a friend who's due up for promotion. If it ever gets out that I leaked some information to you, how's that going to look?"

"A lot better if an important arrest comes out of it."

Morley looked at her closely. He had learned his lesson long ago when it came to disparaging Margaret's little "involvements." Behind her lace collars and seasonal gifts of molasses crisp cookies beat the soul of a thirty-year veteran cop, as tough as an Irish foot patrolman in Little Italy, and as dogged as a Mountie in a Saskatchewan blizzard. So he leaned back in his chair, left off thinking about his new Naugahyde upholstery for a few minutes, and said, "You want to tell me about it?"

"Not yet," she answered. "But when I get more I will. The name's Lazarre, Victor Lazarre. I just want to know if you have anything on him."

Morley sighed and stood up. "If I could read the stock market like I could read you, Margaret, I'd be a millionaire. You come in here maybe once a month, and once a month there's always some polite request for Lieutenant Morley to do. 'Please make sure Burger King cleans up outside their restaurant, Lieutenant Morley. Please have the street lights fixed at the Seventy-ninth Street entrance to Riverside Park, Lieutenant Morley.' What am I, your private ombudsman?"

"So you'll do it then?" Margaret asked with a friendly expression.

Morley threw up his hands in exasperation. "Jesus Christ, I got a choice?" He looked at her for another moment sitting at his desk, her hands folded neatly in her lap.

"You want to wait? It might take a while."

"No problem," she said.

"Just shows you," he added. "And I thought this day was starting out well."

It came back sooner than they expected. In fifteen minutes there was a computer printout on Morley's desk headed by a lot of strange symbols and meaningless letter combinations. The only thing that stood out were the words *Lazarre*, *Victor*. To Margaret, the several lines of following text also looked like they were in Greek. Morley had to translate it for her.

"Your boy, it turns out, has had his day in court. In January, 1972," he said. "The action was brought by someone called Fine Gemstones Inc. Case was disposed through a fine and probation. Probably also a hefty settlement with the plaintiff." Morley looked up. "Here's a case number if you want to get specifics, but that you got to pull off of the microfilm down at the records bureau. Probably take you all day." He scribbled something on a piece of paper and handed it to her. "After that, nothing. I guess he learned his lesson. The thing's dead and buried now over seventeen years."

Margaret grinned. "But still valuable in the right hands." She stood up slowly. "Thank you, Sam." She patted his hand. "You always did have a good heart under the gruff exterior."

"Hey, if you're going down to the records bureau, don't tell them where you got the tip."

"Not to worry, I have a better way to get that information." She turned and headed out the door. Morley watched her leave, wishing he had gone out for a test drive in the new car. He'd have to talk to McSweeney. Next time he wanted some warning before the duty sergeant sent her back.

Twenty-seven

"YOU SURE YOUR FRIEND SAID MR. FEINstein now works for Intercontinental Diamond Company?"

"That's right," Ryker said. "It's in the back. Come on, watch that Eric doesn't bump into all these glass cases."

Margaret continued to follow Ryker through one of the busiest exchanges on the street. Forty-seventh was to diamonds what Broadway was to broken dreams, and most of the action was concentrated in the street-level exchanges, lobby-sized spaces laid out in mazes of tiny booths. The square-foot rental on these pixels of capitalism rivaled the going rates on Fifth Avenue, but if jewelry was your game, Forty-seventh Street was the arena. The booths closer to the front, the ones catering to the retail window shoppers, had their street shills and were the busiest. As Margaret ushered Eric through the aisles she beheld a profusion of gold chains, hundreds of rings, kilograms of precious stones, and enough leering salesmen to make her clutch her pocketbook tighter. Underneath the gloss of decorum and mannered business transactions, these exchanges gave nothing away to a market in a Bedouin village. Mention that you might be interested in something simple, like a holiday gratuity for your manicurist, and you took your life in your hands.

But Margaret and Ryker were not on a buying expedition, at least not for anything you could wear. Old Man Feinstein was still dealing stones even though his own company, Fine Gemstones Inc., had long since gone belly-up. Ryker's informant on the street had at least come through with that much. But Feinstein knew where the hatchet was buried, and maybe, for old times' sake, he'd be willing to give it a twist.

Intercontinental Diamond Company was a good deal smaller than its eloquent title would indicate. Housed in a space perhaps eight by twelve feet, it consisted of a vault on the back wall, two back-to-back metal desks with inexpensive chairs on casters, and a counter that acted as both a showcase and barrier. On the desks were two fluorescent lamps, an electronic scale, some scattered books, and a newspaper. Matzoh crumbs dusted the surface between two empty coffee containers. Cecil B. Rhodes would not have been impressed with these practitioners of the industry he helped found.

"Mr. Feinstein?" Margaret asked tentatively.

The man leaning back in the chair, glanced up from the newspaper, and gave her a once-over.

"You want Feinstein?"

Margaret nodded.

"He'll be right back. He went to return a stone on memo. Wait a bit." He lowered his head again and continued reading.

Eric pounded on the glass in front of him. There were all those pretty glittery things. The noise made the man behind the counter look up again. "So what's the rush? If you don't want to wait for Moe, I can show you too."

Margaret shook her head. "Sorry. That's my little boy. We're not really here to buy anything."

The man looked down through the counter and saw Eric. "So come in. You didn't tell me you had a little *bubulah* with you. Come in." He bent over and reached in his drawer and picked out the biggest diamond Margaret had ever seen. It was easily the size of a golf ball. He held it out to Eric, who was drawn to it as if it were a magnet. "Don't worry, it's just a glass replica. We used it for a promotion a few years back as a paperweight. Oh, here you are, Moe." He looked over Ryker's shoulder. "Some people to see you."

Moe Feinstein came into the little enclosure and looked at them carefully. A black man, an old lady, and a toddler . . . this didn't add up to a sale, not in a million years, so he just shrugged and slid into his chair by the other desk. He looked out at them through a pair of wireframe glasses that had a little loupe attached. He had a tired expression on his face, ably assisted by an electric razor that was as inconsistent as a push mower from the forties. A gray thatch of hair on his head matched the color of his rumpled polyester jacket. The only spot of color on the man was his tie, a red paisley clip-on job.

"Can we have a few words with you, Mr. Feinstein?" Margaret asked.

"Go ahead," he said. "I got until sundown."

"Do you remember a man by the name of Lazarre?" Margaret asked. "Victor Lazarre?"

Feinstein's eyes narrowed perceptibly. He looked from Margaret to Ryker, then down to the little boy playing with the big rock.

"What about Lazarre?"

"I believe you had some trouble with him back in seventy-two." Margaret said.

"It was a long time ago," Feinstein answered.

"Go ahead and tell them, Moe," the other man said. "Once a *momzer*, always a *momzer*. You've been grumbling about him for years."

"What the hell," Feinstein said and leaned back. "You know how Victor Lazarre got his start . . . before he got his in with DeBeers? I'll tell you, by stealing. But not in bits and pieces, mind you. The man was a wholesale goniff. You know what goniff means?"

Ryker looked blank.

"A thief. And did he rob me. Until I found out, he must'a beat me for close to fifty thousand. And I probably wasn't the only one."

"How?" Margaret asked.

"By switching goods. I mean, I checked, but when you buy parcels of two hundred carats of melée or full cuts, you can't look at every stone. That's close to four thousand tiny stones. You take a sample. Depending on how much you trust . . ." he shrugged, "tells you how much to sample. Me, I was a schlemiel, I sampled maybe seventy, maybe a hundred stones. I should have checked a lot more—a lot more," he emphasized. "I was socking the stuff into inventory against a price rise. I think maybe I bought two more big parcels from Lazarre." He shook his head. "Then one day I sell a small lot of it to a jeweler had to make up this big necklace full of pavé. Comes back to me—this is maybe two months later after the mounting is made—and he says half the stones I sent him are CZs."

"CZs?" Margaret said.

"Cubic zirconium," Feinstein replied. "Worthless compared to diamonds. I couldn't believe it so I went back and checked what I had in inventory. Would you believe—" he slapped his forehead, remembering again the disaster—"half of what I had from Lazarre was that junk. Maybe a hundred carats of it. So I called him up and told him to get the hell over and take a look at what he had shipped me and you know what the *momzer*, that son of a bitch says, you'll pardon the expression, he says there's nothing off-grade in what he shipped and if there is, then I must have substituted it. Can you believe the chutzpah!"

There was silence for a minute while Feinstein shook his head. Noises of haggling from the next booth did little to draw Margaret's attention away. Finally she asked, "What did you do?"

"I had the bastard arrested." Now Feinstein broke out into a smile. "He didn't know it, but a friend of mine knew the guy Lazarre was buying the CZs from. I got a copy of the invoice and all—same quantity. I had him cold."

"So how was it settled?" the other salesman said.

Feinstein shrugged. "He didn't want it getting around the street. I think he was just getting involved with DeBeers then. We arranged some deal through our lawyers. I did pretty good. And he got a hefty fine." He took a deep breath. "And that's your Mr. Lazarre."

Ryker looked at Margaret with a frown. "It's a little above YBA's head."

"It'll do," she said.

She held her hand out for the glittery stone Eric was rolling on the soiled piece of carpet in back of the showcase. "Time to go," she said firmly.

"That's all right, lady. You can let him keep the replica. They're cheap enough." Moe's partner opened the drawer to show her maybe half a dozen more.

"Eric, thank the nice man," she said.

The little boy looked from one to the other, then pulled

himself up and walked the two steps towards Margaret. He held his hand out and gave her the stone.

"What is it a replica of?" Ryker asked.

"The Jubilee," Moe Feinstein said. "Two hundred and forty-five carats."

Margaret felt its weight once or twice and then put it in her big pocketbook. "Not something you'd want to wear around your finger," she joked, then turned to Feinstein. "Thank you."

"If it's to screw Lazarre, anytime. Good luck."

Margaret took Eric's hand and began threading her way out of the exchange. When they were back on the street Ryker held her back for a moment.

"What's next?"

"I think I'm ready for Mr. Victor Lazarre; that is, after a hot cup of tea. Then, after that, Charles Wright."

"What about Eric?" Ryker asked.

"I recommend chocolate milk and *Pat the Bunny*," she said. "You'll find it in his bag."

"Me? I'm coming with you."

"No, I've got to do this by myself. The last thing I want is for the Lazarres to get another glimpse of Eric. Sorry, Peter," she said. "You've been appointed nanny for the next few hours."

Ryker looked down at the little boy and picked him up. "Hey, no problem. We're old buddies by now, right, Eric? What's it matter if I'm supposed to be working today."

"Don't worry, Peter, one hand washes the other," Margaret said cryptically.

"What's that supposed to mean? You got something out of those names you lifted?"

"Patience, Mr. Ryker."

"Patience is one thing," he said, "*Pat the Bunny* is quite another."

Twenty-eight

VICTOR LAZARRE'S SMALL ADVERTISEMENT in the Yellow Pages belied the nature of his establishment. Located on Forty-seventh Street just west of Sixth Avenue, Lazarre had two floors with an internal staircase and enough plush carpet to soundproof the reading room of the New York Public Library. All of it was mauve, to go with the teal-tinted entranceway mirrors and the receptionist's pale gray marble desk. This all came after the double set of electronically locked doors that separated this world of extravagant precious stones from the poor working slobs on the street. Once inside, Margaret didn't have long to wait. After a minute the young girl at the desk pointed her in the direction of a large door. Inside, Lazarre was waiting behind one of the prettiest antique desks Margaret had ever seen. However, if friendliness was a commodity, from the looks of his icy stare he had sold short.

"I can give you only a few minutes," Victor Lazarre said. "Sit down."

Margaret marched across the soft carpet and sat in a chair that looked like it cost more than a new car. Louis something or other. She placed her handbag carefully in her lap, then looked up into the diamond dealer's eyes.

"I would like to send you Mr. Feinstein's regards, but they were not offered. He did offer me, however, a long and rather interesting story about his earlier dealings with you."

"Feinstein . . . ?" Lazarre rolled the name over in his mind for a moment. "Oh yeah, but that's old history," he said, turning narrowing eyes on his elderly visitor. "If you think it has any bearing on our adopting Eric Williams . . ."

"Not directly anyway. But I would imagine it does have some bearing on your relationship with the DeBeers people. I hardly think they want it known that one of their favored customers has a history of manipulating diamond scams."

"That was merely a misunderstanding that was all settled peacefully long ago." He tried to sound nonchalant. "Settled and forgotten."

"Not by Feinstein."

"What is this?" Lazarre said leaning forward in his chair. "Are you threatening me?"

"I'd like to think of it as a warning, Mr. Lazarre. Yes, that sounds so much better, don't you think?" Margaret smiled. "DeBeers . . . well you know how stuffy and English they are . . . how much they try to avoid messy scandals." She held his eyes for a moment, then leaned back into the hand-dyed silk fabric of the designer chair. "Yes, a warning."

Lazarre looked at her for a long time without saying anything.

"You know, there are many children out there for adoption," Margaret finally went on. "Perhaps you'll make wonderful parents for another child, but I really think, under the circumstances, you should reconsider becoming Eric's."

Lazarre shook his head slowly, almost imperceptibly, from side to side. "Mrs. Binton," he began, "I didn't get to where I am by taking orders or responding to blackmail threats no matter what you call them. DeBeers and I have been doing business together long enough so that the gossip and prattling of an old lady will be met with laughter. You're barking up the wrong tree. Now if you'll excuse me . . ."

"Certainly," Margaret said standing up. "But I have more gossip than that, gossip about bribes to employees of adoption organizations to purchase healthy white babies. I don't think that kind of gossip is met with laughter, Mr. Lazarre, not if it's backed up with the kind of facts that makes a newspaper decide it's a little more than just an old lady's prattling."

Lazarre swung back in his chair and watched as she stood up. His eyes held a little less of the self-assurance of a few moments earlier, but he didn't make a move to stop her.

"You don't really think you're going to keep the kid, do you?" he said as she reached the door.

"Long enough to see that he's not disposed of like an item in a year-end sale. It's your decision, Mr. Lazarre, whether you want to bow out gracefully or get burned." She turned the handle and the door glided inward. "Do make up your mind soon. The final hearing's in a few days. All it takes is a simple phone call to the YBA."

"Not so simple, Mrs. Binton, after a two-year wait."

"I suppose not, and I suppose not especially after thirty thousand dollars."

Lazarre watched numbly as she closed the door softly behind her. As far as he was concerned, it wasn't so much the money, it was facing up to Susan with the decision. Hell, he thought, there had to be another solution.

Twenty-nine

CHARLES WRIGHT'S OFFICE WAS LARGER than Helen Regency's, but still not the kind of space in which you could lean back, put your feet up, and contemplate how good the world has been to you. Besides the desk and chairs, there was a small table, a filing cabinet, and a standing bookcase. The walls had a bunch of photographs of politicians shaking hands with assorted bureaucrats, which on closer inspection revealed Mr. Wright's face somewhere in the background. In one he was lucky enough to be the recipient of the handshake, but Margaret had no idea who was on the other end of it. She had time to contemplate the decorations since Mr. Wright had been on the telephone for five of the past six minutes since Margaret had taken her seat. Finally the director put the receiver back on the hook and looked up at his visitor.

"I expect you've come to discuss the hearing. I can assure you, Mrs. Binton, while we always try to be fair with all our foster parents, it seems to me that you have given Mrs. Regency enough problems to turn her hair gray." He chuckled at his own lame cliché but it did nothing to soften Margaret's expression.

"Mr. Wright," Margaret began. "I came today to ask you to cancel the hearing altogether, or at the very least, postpone it until certain things are clarified. There's a storm brewing and I don't want to see Eric caught up in it because of bad timing."

"A storm?" Mr. Wright said with some sarcasm. "The only storm I foresee is if you continue to stand in the way of finding Eric a permanent home."

Margaret reached into her oversized handbag and withdrew the small tape recorder. She placed it on the desk in front of her and pushed the play button. Immediately the conversation she had with Amanda's grandmother while baking gingerbread cupcakes reeled out. She stopped the machine after the sequence about the payoff to Mrs. Regency. There was silence in the room for a few seconds.

"As director of this organization, you might be concerned over such an allegation. I can assure you the tape is genuine and admissible in court, as I was the other person. I'm sure you recognized my voice. Now, I am assuming you had no knowledge of Mrs. Regency's little profiteering scheme, but the way you handle things now that you do know will certainly affect your future." Margaret gestured to the pictures on the wall. "I'd hate to see all those good years wind up in the trash heap. Regardless of what you do about Eric, I plan to give a copy of this tape to a reporter friend of mine. That's the storm I am referring to. You can see why at the very least, a delay on his disposition would be the wisest thing for everyone."

Mr. Wright looked stunned. He eyed the little tape recorder as if it were some evil and poisonous thing. Finally he turned his eyes to the woman in front of him. "And do you think the Lazarres are involved in these payoffs?"

"I have no proof of that," Margaret said. "But under the circumstances, I think it highly likely."

Mr. Wright nodded once, then glanced up at the walls with all the photographs of him plodding through the bureaucratic wilderness. "Yes," he said. "I expect it would be hard to get proof of any of it." Then he looked back at Margaret. "I have to make some phone calls," he said finally, "before I make a decision. I'm afraid I can't guarantee anything."

"I understand," she said.

"Thank you for bringing this to my attention." He stood up. "I believe little Eric has a medical appointment later this week?"

"He does, tomorrow. I have it on my calendar."

"Good, I'll let you know about the hearing." He gave her another weak smile and then watched as she exited the small office. After the door closed he sank back down in his seat and pulled the phone closer. *Damn*, he thought, *what a mess.*

He dialed and waited three rings. When the voice on the other end came on he started talking without a break, trying to repeat the entire interview verbatim. He didn't get off the phone for twenty minutes and when he did, he was satisfied that the problem could be contained. At least that's what he had been told.

Thirty

MARGARET FOUND THE TWO OF THEM in their favorite playground playing a game of "Digging to China"—at least that's what Ryker called it. By all accounts Eric was still a long way off but quite determined. Ryker sat on the edge of the six-inch hole in the sandbox and urged him on. Next to both of them was a five-foot stuffed pink panther.

"Who's your new friend?" Margaret asked.

"Hey, it's been over two hours," the reporter said. "After we rubbed the fur off *Pat the Bunny* some guy came by selling these things so I figured I'd lay in another supply. Where've you been?"

Margaret sat down heavily on one of the tire swings. "Thank you, Peter, that was very generous." She grabbed onto a supporting chain with one hand and rubbed her knee with the other. "Everything is all set," she said. "Now it's your turn."

"How's that?"

"You are about to get one of the hottest stories of the year. I can give you names, figures, and everything."

"Damn, you got someone to talk."

"Yes, and on tape."

Ryker smiled up at her. "Margaret, you just saved my life. I thought I was going to have to file my next story on playground politics. Regency's in it?"

"Up to her neck. You got a pencil and paper?"

"I did," he said. "Until I started drawing all the characters from Sesame Street for Eric. Let's go, this can't wait."

"Certainly not until Eric makes it to Peking." She bent down and grabbed the little boy's hand while Ryker picked up the large stuffed animal. Together, the four of them headed out of the park toward Broadway.

Thirty-one

LATER THAT AFTERNOON, HELEN REGENCY slipped into the Jacuzzi and felt her body relax in the warm frothy water. This was always the best part about her visits to the health club. The exercise classes and the jogging treadmill helped her keep in shape, but the hot tub was what really brought her in day after day. It was just so damn luxurious, so . . . Hollywood. She spread her arms out to the side and felt the little bubbles travel up the contours of her body, right up to the halter strap on her bikini, where they leapt off and popped to the surface. Naked, of course, would have been better, but this was a coed Jacuzzi next to the coed pool so she had to make some compromises. She leaned her head against the side of the tub and closed her eyes. A terrific way to finish off a hard day at the office. It wasn't easy dealing with all those foster parents, demanding their goddamn Pamper supplement on top of tokens for the subway, not to mention the little brats themselves, who had to be jollied for the hour they had their medical or spent with their natural parents. Not easy at all. But it had its rewards, it certainly did, and the Eighth Avenue Health and Aerobics Club and especially its Jacuzzi was one of them. She reached out with her right foot and found a jet on the bottom of the tub and let it massage her instep, then her ankle. Just glorious. She closed her eyes and let the bubbles continue their work.

She felt, rather than heard, the other person enter the Jacuzzi. The water level rose about an inch, then filtered out the scuppers until it was back to its normal height. She opened her eyes and nodded at the friendly looking man across from her. She didn't recognize him, but the club had so many members nowadays she hardly knew them all. He had a pleasant face, bright eyes, an unusually wide chin.

"Been in long?" he asked.

She gave him a languid grin, part melted that way from the heat of the tub, and part just because you never knew what things could develop in such a friendly atmosphere.

"About five minutes," she answered. "Hot enough for you?"

"Plenty," he said and slipped down a little lower. All she could see of him was his head and his brush crewcut. She let her glance wonder over to the right in the direction of the pool. She had stayed late today and there weren't too many people still in the club. A couple of women were doing laps and a young man was just toweling off on his way to the lockers. She looked back at the man in front of her but he already had his eyes closed. *What the hell,* she thought. She closed her eyes too and reached out with her other foot for the jet.

The next thing she felt was so entirely out of context she couldn't get her bearings at first. Someone was pulling her hands. She opened her eyes just in time to see the man with the square-cut chin before she was pulled underwater. But the pressure on her arms didn't cease. She was being forced down and now that her mouth was under water, it was too late to scream. The only thing to see as his powerful hands found her shoulders were the thousands of little bubbles dancing before her eyes, bubbles that even in her death struggle curled up her body like tiny shiatsu fingers. She fought for the best part of a minute but she was no match for his whole weight bearing down on her shoulders. The Jacuzzi frothed just a little more than usual, hardly detectable, and from the swimming pool it looked just like a man standing in the center rubbing his knees. But no one was watching, and no one noticed when Helen Regency surfaced again and was propped back in her blissful position with her head against the edge of the tub, her arms outstretched, her eyes closed. The man with the square chin got out of the tub and disappeared into the men's locker room. The time was seven-thirty.

At nine o'clock when they were closing the club someone noticed that Mrs. Regency was still in the hot tub. They turned off the jets and the bubbles and told her it was time to go. The police got the call ten minutes later.

Thirty-two

THE NEXT MORNING, ERIC BREEZED through his monthly medical exam. The nurse-practitioners knew their jobs well and treated both Eric and Margaret with consideration. Once again they proclaimed him healthy, happy, and two pounds heavier. Margaret joked that it must be the escargots in garlic and butter sauce she was feeding him. The nurses had taken her first so it was still early when she left the clinic; neither Wright or Regency was in. By Margaret's reasoning it was also too early to meet any of her friends uptown. The day was mild and bright. She checked her watch again, then made a quick decision. It was only a block to the river, then three down to Forty-sixth. She bent over the stroller and stroked Eric's cheek.

"How about a treat, young man, how would you like to see a big boat?"

"Boot," he repeated with a smile.

"Good, I thought so. It's called the Intrepid. Too big for your bathtub, I'm afraid, but you'll like it anyway." She leaned against the stroller and headed in the direction of the Sea-Air-Space Museum.

A man with a brush cut and square jaw detached himself from a doorway across the street and leisurely followed behind them. He had been waiting since eight o'clock and now had only to wait a little longer . . . just until she got alone somewhere. It wouldn't take long, maybe sixty seconds and she'd be history too like the other one. The man allowed himself a little grin. Five thousand dollars before coffee break—not a bad morning's work at all.

Margaret kept to Eleventh Avenue until she hit Forty-sixth then started down the long industrial block toward the large floating museum. Just ahead of her was a small group of Japanese tourists who were apparently headed in the same direction and taking pictures all around. Not that there was much to see on the block full of garages and warehouses. She lagged behind about twenty yards, struggling with the stroller over the uneven pavement. There was someone behind her, but she paid no attention. She noticed one of the Japanese tourists turn and take a picture of the block behind him, and then the footsteps at her rear seemed to drop back. A few minutes later she crossed under the old West Side Highway elevated structure and found herself in front of the admissions booth at the base of the gigantic ship.

Eric was dazzled at the sight. Nine hundred feet long and over one hundred feet above the water, the World War II aircraft carrier towered over them. Its blunt, T-shaped bow carried an anchor that looked heavy enough to sink a Staten Island ferry. It was a wall of gray, hull and superstructure, blocking off all of downtown Manhattan and much of the sky. Margaret bought a ticket and headed for the handicapped elevator entrance. The Japanese had chosen to walk and Margaret waited patiently for the door to close. As it started inward a hand began to reach around, but the person was too late. The doors shut quickly as Margaret tried to find the "door open" button. By the time she pressed it, the elevator was already on the way.

They emerged onto the hangar deck into a space full of modern planes and missiles. Everything was oversized. On the walls she noticed huge macaroni-shaped catapult steam ducts looking like enormous aortas. A single thought flashed through her mind—Geppetto inside Monstro's stomach. She pushed on to the nearby Carrier Operations Theater, where a motion picture was already in progress. There were several people inside the large darkened room watching modern jets scream across the screen. Eric seemed quite at home with the noise level and so they stayed there for the ten minutes it took until the end of the show. Then they followed the crowd as it headed into the other large areas of the indoor exhibition.

Eric seemed to love the war planes and the decommissioned

anti-aircraft guns scattered around like so many giant's toys. But Margaret's favorite was a smaller section given over to memorabilia from the forties: *Life* magazine covers, wartime fashions, war-bond posters, and a life-size mannequin of F.D.R. How Oscar had loved the man . . . A flood of memories hit her: the fireside chats, the elegant long face with the cigarette in its insouciant little holder . . . Eleanor. Margaret lingered so long that she found the large group had left her. There was only one man left with his back toward her. She hurried out and passed the funniest picture, one of tiny Johnny Philip Morris astride one of the biggest guns on the USS *Missouri*, his uniform and little page's cap still in place. "Call for Philip . . . Morrrrrriss." She remembered the little man's litany so well. It had been her cigarette, and half of America's at the time. Filterless with a kick like a mule. She caught up with the group as they were getting onto the escalator for the flight deck.

The sight of the open space, the size of three football fields, was staggering. There were close to twenty aircraft of all different types—helicopters, fighter jets, rescue amphibians, bombers, trainers, early warning craft. It was an airplane buff's dream, and the large group Margaret was following fanned out to take it all in. Eric was beside himself looking at all the sleek shapes. Margaret left the stroller by a Sikorsky Sea Bat and together they toddled hand in hand around a half dozen of the planes. Eric felt the tires and stared at the big exhaust holes of the jet engines. Margaret just wondered at the sheer power they all seemed to radiate. There was always someone nearby, gawking, touching, pointing. No detail went unnoticed. Everything was so real . . . right down to a pilot's oxygen mask Margaret spotted in one cockpit. You'd almost think some of the planes had just landed. After fifteen minutes Margaret overheard someone mention seeing the command bridge and combat stations inside what was called the "island" and went off with Eric to find the staircase.

Fortunately she was wearing her Dr. Scholls with the rubber soles. The staircase leading up to the bridge was at such a steep angle that Margaret had all she could do keeping Eric in front of her and herself from falling, but they made it up the first flight to the old radio room. It took her a few moments to catch her breath in the dimly lit space. Around her was the ship's old communications center, big gray consoles with numerous black knobs and metal toggle switches, all of them scratched with broken dials and exposed and ripped wiring. But even in its state of disrepair, the communication center lent a feeling of reality and immediacy to the room, as though, like the planes below, this ship and this radio room had lived through history, not merely represented it. Margaret heard footsteps on the metal stairs and decided to move out of the small room. She picked Eric up and stepped gingerly over a watertight door. The corridor outside led past a series of rooms, branched off twice, and then ended in a catwalk that ran along the far side of the center command island and itself ended in a large and menacing anti-aircraft gun. The catwalk was about five feet wide, made of heavy metal mesh, and had a screened-in railing alongside its outer edge. Margaret looked over and down about six stories to the surface of the water below. Instinctively she grabbed onto Eric's hand, although there was no way he could climb the four feet to the top edge of the protective railing.

They were the only ones on the catwalk so it was easy for them to move along it to the large gun turret. Margaret lifted Eric into the gunner's seat of the four-barrelled, forty millimeter Quad where he sat, quite contentedly, pulling a worn brass lever back and forth. Margaret leaned against the railing and rubbed one of her calves.

"This is as far as we go, Eric." She looked to her right and saw that the turret at the end of the catwalk was propped slightly outboard a few feet in space. "My legs can't take another staircase and if we don't start heading back soon I'm afraid your stroller might be gone." She had to shout a little to overcome the sound of the wind funnelling up the side of the ship past their exposed position. They were alone on this side of the ship opposite from the flight deck, and quite unobserved. Because of the whistling noise, she didn't hear the man approaching on the steel grating. But she did catch a glimpse of his light green windbreaker and turned to look.

At first all she registered was a mild surprise. The man was still perhaps twenty feet away, but making toward her with a set to his features unusual for a tourist. It was almost as though he had a message for her, or perhaps she had dropped something and he was coming to return it. But then it registered. His face . . . those narrow eyes and wide chin, that brush crew-cut!

Once again she reached out instinctively for Eric, but the little boy was several feet away and holding on tight to the hydraulic levers around him. Margaret took a step forward, but the man was there first, brushing between them.

Then she remembered. The man from the Central Park boating lake, the man who had shot out the bottom of their boat. She put a hand up to her throat to scream, but his hand got there first and clamped down over her mouth.

"I told you, lady, to stop messing around in other people's business, but you wouldn't listen—"

Margaret managed to utter a short sentence before his crushing hand squeezed her lips closed.

"Don't hurt the boy."

"Oh no, the boy has a long future ahead of him. I'm sorry I can't say the same for you." He looked around quickly to make sure they were alone, then reached out a hand toward Margaret's waist. "You're gonna take a little swim," he continued, "after a long dive. They'll think you leaned over too far. And when you come up, you won't even need that hospital ship over there." He started awkwardly lifting her, one hand still over her mouth, the other around her body. As her feet came off the ground, her right hand clutched for the railing and the other reached around her assailant's neck, trying to hold on.

At the sight of Margaret struggling with the unknown man, Eric stopped playing with his knobs and levers and just stared. A look of worry came over his face, and slowly, very slowly, he started to cry. The noise floated away on the wind current, a noise not unlike the cries of other babies to have visited the warship who were either tired or hungry or wet. It did nothing to stop the man from continuing to lift Margaret up to the level of the protective railing. A few more seconds, the man thought, then he'd quickly disappear into the maze of the huge ship and exit with one of the groups. One more push . . .

Except Margaret wasn't moving. The grip she had on the railing and around his neck was strong enough to counteract the one arm he was using to lift her. He tried to jiggle loose her handhold, pulling this way and that, but she held on tenaciously. Her handbag, still around the wrist over his shoulder, banged against the railing and snapped open, spilling out her compact, the Bic lighter, and the folded morning crossword puzzle. This was getting messy, her assailant thought, and taking too long. He'd have to use two hands and chop her grip off the railing. He lowered her just a few inches to get a better hold on her waist and took his hand away from her mouth. Margaret saw his karate chop coming, and took her hand off the railing just in time. His hand sliced harmlessly through the air where her wrist had just been and he cursed, but she no longer had a grip on anything solid. He took a half step back and took the railing out of her reach. A tiny grin crossed his face as he saw the panic in her eyes. But Margaret wasn't looking at him. She was staring into the open handbag hanging over his shoulder and at her one last chance. As she felt him lifting her again, this time with both muscular arms, she reached in, fumbled for a split second, and withdrew the heavy glass replica of the Jubilee diamond that Feinstein's partner had given her.

She was over him now, his head and face quite unprotected, and in one arcing motion with her free hand she brought the point of the fake diamond down with all her adrenalin-crazed energy on the bridge of his nose. The two hundred and forty-five carats concentrated on one four-square-millimeter culet was too much for the soft cartilege of her assailant's nose. He screamed in pain and brought his right hand up to his nose. Blood began frothing from his nostrils and made the lower half of his face look like Carmen Basilio's in his last title fight. But Margaret wasn't finished with the Jubilee. She brought it down again, this time on the crown of his head, and for good measure, gave him a forehand to his temple. Which of the two blows dropped him was hard to say, but he slumped on the metal grating, limp as a sack of turnips. His hands twitched for a few seconds, then he was still. Margaret finally found her voice and screamed. She was leaning against the railing with the blood-stained glass paperweight in her hand and for a few seconds her sounds mixed with Eric's cries. Then abruptly she stopped, stepped over the fallen man, and reached out for the little boy.

"It's all right, Eric, he can't hurt us any more." She could feel her heart pounding, the adrenaline still working its magic. She felt lightheaded, about to faint, but she knew she had to hold on, if only for Eric's sake. She steadied herself against the gun carriage and took a series of deep breaths. Ten seconds, maybe fifteen went by, but it felt like a year. Then she heard a noise on the catwalk behind her and turned to see a man running toward her. He had on a uniform, some kind of security-guard thing with a lot of gold and blue braid, with no gun belt, but with plenty of muscle. She was never so glad to see another person in her whole life.

Thirty-three

"OKAY, SO MAYBE NOW YOU WANT TO tell me about it?'' Morley said. ''I mean you almost kill some guy, he's in the hospital with a broken nose and a concussion, and they pick you up with some little kid, no less . . .'' Lieutenant Morley pulled a cigarette out of his pack and flipped one across the desk to her. ''Kurmansky down at the Fourteenth says you wouldn't go into the fine points until you talked to me. So okay,'' he repeated. ''I'm listening. Was it that guy Lazarre?''

She shook her head. ''I don't know who it was, Sam, but he tried to kill me—twice.'' She lit her cigarette and held the match for the lieutenant. ''Well once, really. The first time he just put a few bullets through the boat I was in.''

''Jesus Christ, Margaret. You have a knack for making life interesting. What the hell did he shoot at you for?''

''Because I was onto this operation of selling babies. Did I tell you I became a foster mother?''

Morley didn't blink, didn't even move his eyes. ''Must have been one of those little details you forgot to mention. Was that the kid?''

Margaret nodded. ''Eric. He's now at the nursery with some of my friends. I only hope he forgets what happened this morning.''

''The guy you put in the hospital probably feels the same way. When he comes around he's probably going to press charges against you.''

''He wouldn't dare. That nice officer Kurmansky told me they had witnesses from the hospital ship. It was plain as day what he was trying to do. If it hadn't been for the paperweight he would have succeeded, too."

"You want to be more specific," Morley said. "And slowly please, Margaret. I don't want to miss anything."

So she started from the beginning and told him everything; about Eric and the Biddies and Kiddies nursery, about Ryker, Regency, Wright, and the Lazarres, about Lucky Haynes and Amanda's grandmother, Mrs. Constance Stafford-Park. When she was finished she waited for some reaction.

Morley frowned. "Did you say Regency?"

Margaret nodded.

"Hold on." Morley flipped through some papers on his desk and came up with the overnight homicide sheet. He ran his finger down the column until he came to it. "Helen Regency. Black woman in her forties, five feet five inches. Social worker employed by the Youth Benevolent Association. Found poached in a Jacuzzi in some West Side health club. Probably drowned, from the look of the bruises around her neck." He dropped the report and looked straight at Margaret. "No suspects at this moment."

Margaret flinched noticeably. She took a deep breath and then said slowly, "That's her."

"Think it could be the same guy?"

"I'd say it was a good bet." She answered. "You got to make sure he stays in that hospital. Show his picture around at the health club. Maybe someone will recognize him." She shook again and this time Morley realized it was from fear. "Could have been me."

"That's what happens when you try to play Lois Lane."

"Thanks." She glowered at him. "This baby selling has been going on for a long time and I didn't notice any police on the case. Don't throw Lois Lane at me, I'll throw Knapp Commission at you."

Morley chuckled but it was strained. He stubbed his cigarette out in the ashtray and leaned forward. "So what do you want me to do? Ask Kurmansky for the case up here? On what grounds?"

"On the grounds Eric and I live in your precinct. On the grounds that you were already investigating the case because of the Central Park attack. Who cares? Kurmansky is okay, but he doesn't know me. And I especially need your help—now."

"Oh?" Morley looked interested. "You have maybe another idea how to follow up? I mean if this guy in the hospital clams up, which is likely."

"I do," Margaret said. "But I can't do it, and my friend Ryker can't either. He's already been up to Lucky's."

"Lucky's?" Morley repeated.

"Yes," Margaret said. "It's time to put a little heat on Mr. Damon Haynes."

Thirty-four

AFTER OVER THIRTY YEARS ON THE NEW York police force there was little Morley could do about it; he looked like a cop, he walked like a cop, and to the people with any street smarts he even smelled like a cop. It wasn't just the polyester and brogans, or the way he leaned forward a little more than normal when he walked, it was the eyes again. It was the way they casually sifted every detail of his environment like an airline pilot before takeoff. And of course it was the gun, tacked unimaginatively to his waist, where it bulged out his paunch asymmetrically and as much as announced his profession. The hell, he was a cop and proud of it. The last thing he was going to do was try and hide it.

Damon Haynes took it all in the space of a heartbeat and nodded him into his office. He was used to all types, undercover rookies, flat-out patrolmen, sergeants, detectives, and even the occasional precinct commander. This one was like all the other ones, an attitude a mile high and an ego to match. Came with the territory. The only good thing was that they all had their price. Lucky sank into his desk chair and flipped his hand up.

"How can I help you?"

Morley let his eyes travel around the expensively furnished office before answering.

"Nice place you got here. Business must be good."

"I do all right," Lucky said. "But if you're selling something I already made some contributions to my friends up at the Eighteenth."

"Selling?" Morley shook his head. "Not selling, Lucky, buying. You know someone by the name of Helen Regency?"

If Lucky did he wasn't letting on. He furrowed his brow, made a show of thinking, then shook his head. "I'm afraid you got me."

"Not yet, asshole, but I will if you keep up the innocent routine. I'm not here on some insurance claim or petty heist. And I'm not here to stick you up for a few hundred because I'm late with my Christmas club. Helen Regency was murdered yesterday. It's the kind of crime the DAs get pretty riled up about. I thought you maybe had some ideas."

This time Lucky didn't even bother with the theatrics. He didn't budge from the position he was in. His eyes held Morley's for a good half-minute.

"Why'd you think that?"

"Because there've got to be half a dozen cash tickets in her drawer from your establishment, each with an initial that says D.H. I'm not a betting man, Lucky, but I'd lay down a thousand I could match that signature pretty easily." He leaned back. "Now the way I figure it, you got two choices. You can tell me what you know about what was going down with Regency, or you can kiss this nice little gig you got here good-bye. There are no secrets up in Harlem, Lucky. You're here because you serve certain functions in the community. Some of them are legal . . . and some of them we have to live with. After a while when the ones we have to wink at get out of hand . . ." he shrugged, "we change the players. You understand?"

"Sounds like a threat," Lucky said angrily.

"Yeah, and believe me it wouldn't be hard. One sweep through here would give us enough stuff to put you on ice for a long time. You're a big boy. You understand how the system works." Morley hesitated. "I need some information on how she did things then I'll walk. It's your choice."

Lucky chuckled. "You realize you're cutting right into the heart of my business. Things here are supposed to be confidential."

"What's that mean with someone who's dead? Regency's never going to get the message."

"You have a point there," Lucky said. "But how's it going to look if it gets out?"

"A lot better than if it gets out you're up in Attica and the police are minding the store. A lot better."

Damon Hayes let that sink in for a moment.

"Okay, I knew her. She came in here maybe once a month to make . . . ah, certain deposits."

"How big?"

"Five grand . . . for her account."

"What's that supposed to mean? She brought in stuff for other people?"

"Person," Lucky corrected. "Five for her, and twenty-five, sometimes thirty, for some other guy."

Morley's eyes narrowed. "For whom?"

"It won't do you any good. I told you I sell confidentiality. The other money went into an account for a Mr. Henry D. Bracton. Five for her, the rest for him, always in cash. I never met the guy, and I had no idea where the money came from. I don't ask too many questions; it's not healthy."

"Once a month?" Morley whistled. "For how long?"

"Couple of years. Maybe three."

"You got a total?" Morley asked.

"Now this is really getting heavy. You want specifics."

Morley just looked at him. "You want to sleep in your own bed tonight?"

Lucky sighed and opened a drawer to his right. He got a key out, then stood and went to a wall safe behind him. In a minute he was back with a large notebook. He flipped through it with the skill of a practiced teller until he came to one of the pages in the back. He ran his finger down to the bottom of the page then looked up.

"At this moment, Mrs. Helen Regency has loaned our company a little over forty-two thousand dollars."

"And Mr. Henry D. Bracton?"

"Oh he's up there . . . seven hundred and eighty-two thousand, give or take a few hundred."

Morley eyed the little notebook with contempt. "All of course reported to the IRS."

"I told you I don't ask questions."

"No, I suppose not. And how did Mr. Bracton get his money out of safekeeping?" Morley asked. "Regency?"

Lucky shook his head. "She was authorized only to make deposits, not withdrawals. Of course, her own account she could enter any time she wanted."

"So I noticed from those slips."

"When Mr. Bracton needed cash, he'd send someone in—always the same guy—with a little note. 'Course the guy's name probably wasn't Henry D. Bracton, but the signature was the same all the time. It was the deal Regency worked out when she first came in. Went along pretty smoothly too."

"Until yesterday," Morley added. "Can you describe the guy? I don't suppose he had a name."

"Uh-unh. White, about six foot, medium build, narrow eyes, big goddamn chin and, oh yes, brush crewcut. The guy looked like Joe Palooka in the funnies."

Morley reached inside his jacket pocket and withdrew a black-and-white picture he had made that afternoon. "Like this?"

"Yeah, I suppose that's him. Without the bandages."

Morley nodded. "Good. Now we're getting somewhere. Next I'll need those withdrawal notes. I bet you got them on file?"

"Perhaps. But I'm not about to put my ass in a wringer. First you gotta tell me I'm not going to get burned."

"Oh no, Lucky, not you." Morley sounded disgusted. "You only launder and stash the illegal cash. Nothing wrong in that."

Damon Haynes smiled. "I am just providing a convenient banking service. You going to prove otherwise?"

"You got it figured out pretty good, don't you, Lucky? But don't press it. One day your luck will run out and you'll have to change your name."

"No way man. When that happens I won't need a name, I'll just be dead." He winked at Morley and got up to fetch the receipt.

Thirty-five

ON HIS WAY DOWN TO THE HOSPITAL, Morley thought he'd cover all bases and check in at the Youth Benevolent Association. He wanted to see what the place looked like, maybe talk to some people about Regency. He didn't want to make it formal, not yet.

The receptionist took note of his badge but said Mr. Wright was out anyway. To his next question she answered she would have to get approval if he wanted to take a look at Regency's office.

"She in some kind of trouble?" she asked innocently. "She didn't come in today."

"Not any more," Morley answered succinctly.

"Let's see, Jason Sawyer is usually at his office or one of the other children's agencies in the morning, but I think I saw him here." She checked in her directory, then dialed a number. In a moment she had him on the phone.

"He'll be right down," she said and hung up softly. "He was just on his way out."

In two minutes the attorney emerged from the elevator with a light raincoat on. He was struggling to cram five or six large folders into a sleek briefcase that looked like it would only accept half that number. He got what he could inside and balanced the rest on top.

"Yes?"

Morley introduced himself and motioned him to one side, away from the receptionist. He explained that Helen Regency had been found murdered and that he wanted to take a brief look around.

"Helen Regency." Sawyer's face registered shock. "That's awful. Her boyfriend or something?"

Morley shook his head. "We don't have any leads yet. You mind?"

Sawyer shrugged. "No, go ahead, fourth floor, second office down the hall. I'd go with you but I have to be down-town in court in twenty minutes. Two dispositions from here and a few more from another children's agency in the Bronx. Everyone's caseload in this city is too full."

"Ain't that the truth," Morley said. "Where's Wright to-day?"

"Fund-raising lunch," Sawyer said. "Must be running late."

Morley took a step towards the elevator. "Thanks."

"You find anything let me know," Sawyer called after him, then spun around and headed toward the door.

Regency's office was sort of what Morley expected from Margaret's description; nothing more than a serviceable old desk, a file cabinet, a few chairs, and a bunch of old posters on the wall. Tossing the place would take all of twenty minutes. He didn't really expect to find anything new. Margaret had already uncovered the pawn tickets that he wanted and the rest of it was probably agency business.

Except that he couldn't find the pawn tickets where Margaret had said they were. He picked the tray of pencils up but the narrow space underneath had nothing from Mr. Damon Haynes's establishment, not unless you figured that twenty containers of pure-grade crack had their origin in a pawn shop. Morley whistled and lifted them out. This case was getting to be fun, the kind of fun you used to have working your way through Steeplechase Park with all its contorted mirrors and funny floorboards and compressed air shocks. A barrel of laughs, except he wasn't amused, nor did he think Margaret would be. Helen Regency and drugs . . . that was a new angle. He pocketed the evidence and continued searching. But there were no more surprises and in fifteen minutes he left and headed down to Bellevue Hospital.

Thirty-six

HIS NAME WAS WILLIAM MYRTLE, A VIETnam veteran, honorable discharge in '75. After that he wound up in New York's unskilled labor pool, working as a grocery packer, truck driver, carpenter, and in half a dozen other jobs before he had his first brush with the law. In 1983 he had been busted on an assault charge and spent a few months on Rikers Island. After that he resurfaced on a drug possession rap, did a couple more years, and graduated into the minor leagues of disorganized free-lance crime. It was not hard to believe that the man Morley looked down at in the hospital bed later that morning had finally hired himself out as a killer. The expression "cream always rises to the top" has its corollary in the streets of New York: sooner or later, the dregs hit the bottom. In Myrtle's case, the bottom was going to be an arraignment on a count of murder one and two counts of attempted murder. Not that that had any noticeable effect on the man. He looked up at Morley with an expression that ran the gamut from nonchalance to boredom as he took occasional sips from an apple juice container on the hospital nightstand. Morley knew he was not going to get anything out of this, but he went on with the interview anyway.

". . . Like I said, Myrtle, you're in enough trouble to put you in the slammer for life. Fact is, when you come out, a gay black woman will be president. Think about it. I told you your options."

"Yeah, whynt'cha speak to my lawyer?"

"We got a positive ID from the receptionist at the club," Morley continued, "two people on that hospital ship saw you trying to push Mrs. Binton over the railing, and Mr. Haynes up in Harlem identified you as the bagman for all that illegal cash. You're lawyer is going to be one busy dude. All I'm asking for is the name of your boss and a little cooperation, and I'll see what I can do on some of these charges."

Myrtle leaned back into the pillows. The butterfly bandage was still on his nose and his eyes had more earthtones around them than a Gauguin landscape, but still he managed a smile.

"Yeah, I might have been at that club that day. You trying to tell me that I was the only one there all day? You couldn't get an indictment on that kind of circumstantial evidence if I was Charles Manson. Then do yourself a favor and check how far away that hospital ship was and figure how good that's going to look in court. You got a hell of a nerve trying to make deals when you're holding an empty hand."

"We'll see, Myrtle."

"Besides, when I get out of here this afternoon there's no way you're gonna hold me in detention. I got my bail all lined up and then you can just take your little deals and put the screws to someone else."

Morley didn't say anything for a moment.

"You're being real stupid, Myrtle, but then I suppose that's what got you in trouble in the first place. You think you're boss is just going to let this thing play out?"

"I don't know what you're talking about," Myrtle said. He reached over and grabbed the box of juice again. "Alls I know is I may have said something a little funny to that old lady, and the next thing I know she hits me with this rock. She's the one that should get booked. I'm thinking of suing."

"Sure you are," Morley said disgustedly. This was getting nowhere. He decided to try one last angle.

"Helen Regency had a lot of crack in her possession. You know anything about that. Was she dealing?"

Myrtle shook his head slowly. "What's crack?"

Morley looked at his watch and decided to throw in the towel with this one. "What a dumb son of a bitch you are," he said and turned to walk away.

"We'll see who's so dumb," Myrtle shouted and rose up in bed. He threw the empty juice container at Morley's back, but it didn't make it past the middle of the corridor in front of his bed. By that time, the lieutenant was halfway out the door.

Thirty-seven

AN HOUR LATER, MORLEY PUT IN AN APpearance at the Biddies and Kiddies nursery. Children had never been his strong suit, and collections of them reinforced his notion that schoolteachers should earn as much as mayors. He found it difficult to carry on a conversation with Margaret while one toddler had a grip on his left leg and another was climbing up his back.

"Can't we go upstairs or something?" he asked her irritably. "I wanted to tell you what's happening."

"I can't leave Eric again," she said. "Not even for a few minutes. Alice told me he cried all yesterday afternoon when I was away."

The mountain climber at Morley's back slid down into his lap and pulled on his tie.

"Jason," she said. "Go see Sid. He has a tie on too." She gently picked him off Morley and put him on his feet a few steps away. "They do kind of get in the way of serious conversation," she added when she came back. "Eric will be good." She reached out a hand and the other little boy came over and took it. "I'm glad you finally could meet him. By the way, did you see Ryker's story in today's paper?"

Morley nodded. "They'll have a field day when they get the news about Regency. I expect there'll be some heat coming down." Morley stretched his legs out and leaned back in the tiny kid-sized chair. "Real comfortable seats you got here."

Margaret chuckled. "I told you to lose some weight. So, Mr. Myrtle give you anything?"

"Yeah, he said he's going to sue you. What a circus."

"The fact is Regency's dead, and Eric's still not out of the woods. I got a call this morning from Mr. Wright saying that in view of all the publicity from Ryker, they're putting Eric's adoption on hold. That's the good part."

Morley raised an eyebrow.

"The bad part is that because of my part in all this, they're still planning to remove Eric, this time to another temporary foster home. Under the circumstances, Wright doesn't think the atmosphere at the Binton residence is conducive to Eric's health and well-being. He set up the meeting with the referee in two days and told me if I don't show up there'll be an immediate and final order for Eric's removal. I guess I have no choice." She shook her head. "Seems like you win a couple of battles and the next thing you know you've lost the war." She looked at Morley. "What else from Myrtle?"

Morley shook his head. "I think he'll go down, but not on the murder—not yet, anyway. But Haynes told me something interesting. Regency was mostly a bag lady in this deal. All the while she was collecting quarters for herself she was collecting dollars for someone else. Someone called Henry D. Bracton. Maybe an alias because we don't have anything on anyone by that name."

Margaret frowned. "No, you wouldn't," she said almost to herself.

"You know someone like that?"

"Uh-unh. Was it a lot of money?"

"Close to eight hundred thousand." He reached into his pocket. "All withdrawals made through these little innocuous slips brought in by the silent Mr. Myrtle."

Margaret took them, looked through them casually, then handed them back. A few dropped on the floor and Margaret bent down quickly to scoop them up.

"The way I see it," Morley said, repocketing the slips, "that puts us right in Charles Wright's lap. He was Regency's supervisor, he's jerking your boy Eric around . . . I would say he's due for a visit. By the way, someone at the YBA cleaned out Regency's pawn slips. Instead there was this." He held up one transparent vial of crack. "I don't suppose you saw this when you were looking."

"It wasn't there, I can assure you. You tell Wright about it?"

"He wasn't there. Sawyer was on his way out but he told me to go on up. What do you make of it?"

"A red herring," Margaret said without hesitation.

"It's a strong possibility. I suppose I'm going to have to put a tail on Myrtle."

Margaret turned white. "A tail. You mean he's getting out."

"Under the Constitution of the United States, we can't hold him. There's no clear and persistent danger that if he's released he's likely to skip town and has the means to do so. Bail is only to assure reappearance, Margaret, nothing else."

"Good Lord." Margaret closed her eyes and inhaled deeply. After a minute she finally turned on Morley. "So what's your tail going to produce?"

"You got a better idea?"

"Maybe. What time's the arraignment?"

"There o'clock this afternoon down at 100 Center Street."

"I was thinking maybe I'd go see for myself," Margaret said and pulled Eric closer.

"You crazy?"

"No, just angry."

Thirty-eight

THE PART TWO COURTROOM DOWN AT 100 Center Street was hopping with activity like some throbbing street corner on a warm evening in Bedford Stuyvesant. Guards ushered prisoners to and fro, lawyers danced about making motions as freely as they cracked jokes between themselves, and witnesses, scores of witnesses, cooled their heels behind the spectator's railing, waiting interminable hours to impart their two minutes' testimony. Presiding over this melange was a judge of such machinelike precision that he gave the impression he was singlehandedly trying to obliterate New York's judicial backlog. If he spent more than five minutes on a case one felt the impatience in his stony eyes. His nickname was Enema Ed among his beleaguered clerks, who could always count on Judge Edward Rostinkowski to clear out his daily calendar on time. Today, at precisely three forty-five, Judge Rostinkowski heard the case against one William Myrtle, which included his ruling on Myrtle's bail. As expected, by four o'clock Myrtle was on his way out of the door, his lawyer having made the appropriate motions and posted the required bond.

This little man who argued on Myrtle's behalf looked like the "before" ad for Spray 'n Starch. His shirt was crumpled, his necktie lowered, and his suit as shiny as an upholstered bannister. He knew his job, however, and negotiated Mr. Myrtle through the process with the confidence of a man who has done something too often to make mistakes. He left as unceremoniously as he had appeared, stopping only long enough to make sure his client understood that he was free to go. They exchanged a few words, then Myrtle walked out of the courtroom with a smirk on his still-bandaged face. Margaret noticed a middle-aged man detach himself from underneath one of the nearby doorway arches and start out after him. With the patch of white on his face, Myrtle would be an easy mark in a crowd, if he didn't try anything cute. But that was not Margaret's problem. She wasn't there to doublecheck on Morley's man, but rather to do a little free-lance job on her own. With Eric, of course, because it was a fine afternoon and he needed a walk anyway . . .

Myrtle's lawyer turned right on Center Street and walked steadily north. Margaret followed him, at first about fifty yards back, pushing Eric in the stroller and trying her best to avoid collisions with the increasing pedestrian traffic. A great cover, she figured, if only she could keep up. She found herself dropping back as the streets got more crowded. The little man turned east on White Street and north on Baxter, a street with fewer pedestrians, and Margaret just caught sight of him as he entered a building a half-block ahead. Eric squealed with delight as Margaret almost did a wheelie to catch up and trotted into the building just as the elevator doors were opening.

"Hold it please," she shouted and the little man obliged, politely holding the door until she could make it inside with her giggling child. He smiled at them absently and pushed the button marked sixteen. Margaret pushed eighteen and struggled to catch her breath.

They were in a building of small offices with an even smaller maintenance budget. The elevator walls were scratched, one fluorescent light cover was missing, and the doors slammed shut with the grace of a hydraulic scrap-metal press. Definitely low-rent district, Margaret figured and waited as the elevator rose to drop off the other man. She noted which direction he took upon exiting, then did the round trip up to eighteen. When the door opened again on sixteen the corridor was empty. She pushed Eric out in front of her, turned the way Shiny Suit had gone, and found herself in front of two doors. One was for the accounting firm of Delgado and Gomez and appeared to be locked. The other was for the firm of lawyers of Myers, Skotowski, Beladonna, and Rabin. She could hear a typewriter clicking somewhere inside and the jerky sounds of some rock music filtering out through the glass panel. High-priced Wall Street lawyers they weren't, but then Margaret wasn't expecting anything different. She fumbled in her handbag for a few seconds, then pushed the door open, drawing Eric in behind her.

They must have been used to family clients in the office because the receptionist hardly looked up from her typing. The radio, playing something from Sting, was by her elbow.

"Excuse me," Margaret began. "I was just in the elevator with a gentleman who I think went into this office."

The woman gave her the benefit of a sidelong glance. "Yeah?"

"He must have dropped his pen, because I heard it drop just as he got out. It's a nice pen, take a look." She held it out, her favorite two-dollar Scripto fine-line felt marker, which she used on her crossword puzzles. Well, it was a cheap price to pay for good information. "You could give it to him. You know how people sometimes get attached to things . . ."

The woman sighed and took the pen. "That'll be Rabin. He just walked in. I swear, that man needs a personal valet. Thanks, I'll give it to him." She went back to her typing.

Margaret pushed back through the door and made it into the elevator before Rabin put two and two together. In another minute she was back out on the street and heading toward the subway.

Myrtle breathed into the pay telephone in a voice barely above a whisper. He was in a drugstore on Canal Street and could clearly see the undercover policeman pretending to shop over by the perfumes. Well, what the hell did he expect?

"I gotta see you," he repeated. "We gotta get something straight."

"I told you not to call me again." The voice sounded angry. "I arranged the bail and now it's time for you to disappear."

"It ain't gonna be so easy. I'm in a lot of goddamn hot water here. There's a cop on my ass, and you want to kiss me off with a few thousand bail money." Myrtle sneered. "It's gonna cost you more, a lot more, that is unless you want to get involved. All you have to do is write out another Henry

D. Bracton withdrawal slip for me to give to Lucky, then I'm gone."

There was silence on the line for a moment and Myrtle glanced up at the man tailing him. He was still there but he had moved on now to the candy section.

"Okay, can you lose the cop?"

"Shouldn't be too hard. Where do you want to meet?"

Myrtle listened carefully and smiled. "I always like train stations," he said, "for quick exits. See you there in two hours." He hung up the phone and straightened. Now, about the cop . . . Hell, two hours was enough time to lose an army of cops.

Thirty-nine

SONJA MILLER REMEMBERED THEM WELL, the older woman and the baby, Eric Williams. As a legal aid attorney she saw hundreds of cases a year but there was something special about this one, an odd and memorable mix. And that day-care facility—Biddies and Kiddies it was called—now it all came back. She leaned into her chair and offered Margaret a seat.

"Certainly," she said with a smile. "I have more than a few minutes. After all, Eric is my client."

"I still had your card," Margaret said, "and since I was right down here by the courts, I thought we'd drop in."

"And how is Eric doing," Sonja said, bending down to his level and giving him a little squeeze on the shoulder.

"Well, you know they want to remove me as foster parent?"

The lawyer sighed and straightened up. "I was just notified. I truly hate these things when they happen. They're bad for the children, they're bad for the system." She shook her head. "They should only pull it when the child's safety or health is in doubt. It doesn't look like Eric is suffering too much." She looked up at Margaret. "But you know I already told them that. Unfortunately I don't have any real say in the foster-parent choice since his legal status hasn't changed. I'm just an interested bystander."

"I know that," Margaret said, "but I was wondering if you could do me a small favor . . ." She shook her head. "Actually, it's a big favor, but it's really for Eric."

"If I can," she grinned. " I'd be happy to."

"Well, the way I figured it, all you lawyers down here are

in kind of a friendly fraternity. You know who works on what kind of stuff, who's with what firms, who's having lunch with whom—that kind of thing."

"Not all of it."

"No, but enough. I was interested particularly in one lawyer, a Mr. Leonard Rabin. His office is a few blocks away, over on Baxter. He's with Myers, Skotowski, Beladonna and Rabin." Margaret leaned forward. "Ever hear of them?"

Sonja nodded her head and the long sweep of dark hair swung onto her shoulder.

"Sure, they're kind of a sleazy operation. They handle mostly criminal cases, a lot of DWI stuff. Rabin I think is their courtroom guy. Short, forties, kind of unkempt?"

"That's him."

"Kind of like a hired gun. So?"

"So, today he got someone off on bail who I can't imagine had one hundred dollars saved up, never mind the ten thousand dollars he needed. Rabin doesn't look like a charitable kind of man, so he must be handling the case on behalf of someone else."

"Sounds right."

"I was wondering if there was any way to find out who put up the money."

Sonja Miller frowned. "Unlikely, although lawyers talk shop like anybody else, just not around people they don't know. If he had a big mouth . . ."

"That's what I thought," Margaret smiled. "You know anybody that could get close to Rabin?"

Sonja grinned again. Margaret's lack of subtlety had not been lost on her. "They're over on Baxter, you said?"

Margaret nodded.

"Well, if it's for Eric. There's a bar near there called McGillies. The place is kind of out of the way but a lot of lawyers go there at the end of the day to unburden their souls and tell war stories. Strictly off the record, mind you. A woman lawyer in there has just about carte blanche on any conversation. Not many of them show up and the boys kind of show off a bit when they do." She paused and looked carefully at Margaret. "Now I suppose I could make a detour there tonight, see if he's around . . ."

Margaret gleamed. "Could you really?"

"No promises now, it's a long shot."

"I understand."

"So," Sonja Miller said and picked up a pen. "What's the guy's name he sprang?"

"Myrtle. It was in Judge Rostinkowski's courtroom."

"Hey, no problem," Sonja said. "I clerked for Rostinkowski. I have enough war stories to keep McGillies jumping for hours."

Forty

NELSON EDWARDS HAD BEEN CLEANING Pennsylvania Station for thirty-five years, long before there was an Amtrak Corporation, before there were sushi joints and croissant outlets and all those other cutesie retail shops, and certainly before the plague hit. The plague, as Nelson liked to refer to it, was the onslaught of the homeless. Used to be a time, he remembered, when they were all in one spot called the Bowery, nicely contained, out of people's way. You stayed out of the Bowery, you never had to see them. Now, how could he mop a floor when it was littered with sleeping bodies and scores of filthy shopping bags? And when they weren't in your goddamn way, then they were like roaches, finding all the niches and crannies in the station and winding up in the most forlorn places. One day he found one in the crawl space between a high voltage transformer and the dumpster for track garbage . . . lying there, blissfully asleep no more than two feet from being fried if he touched the wrong piece of metal. But thankfully, for the most part they were harmless, copping a few zzzs and a little warmth, and if they were lucky, a small bit of change.

So Nelson had worked out a routine. If they were in his way, he asked them to move. If they weren't, he passed them by. Very simple. Let the cops handle the political aspect of the situation: field all the complaints from the outraged white-collar executives from Locust Valley and blue-collar workers from Wantaugh, do the unpleasant stuff of bundling them off somewhere, touching them. Ugh! Hey, Nelson thought, live and let live. Why get into hassles with nine more months left before retirement?

Except there was this creep underneath a maintenance stairway that looked kinda funny. Nelson couldn't put his finger on it, but he'd passed him by now three times and the guy hadn't moved an inch. Not only that, his clothes looked like they'd seen the inside of a washing machine in the last week, which was definitely out of the ordinary. And he was at this funny angle . . .

Nelson approached cautiously and kneeled down. The maintenance stairway was hidden from the general public area through a doorway and short corridor. It went down to track number eight and was used sometimes to store things like mopping buckets and cleaning chemicals. It was quiet inside the stairwell, blocked off from everything by its thick concrete walls. Nelson nudged the man's foot with his hand and got no response. Nor did he get anything when he reached up and tapped the man on the shoulder with his mop handle. It was dark in there and Nelson drew back to grab hold of his belt flashlight. He was getting this funny feeling in the pit of his stomach, like the time that drunk slipped onto the tracks and he had gotten stuck doing the cleanup. A nasty, queasy feeling. He switched on the small beam and looked closer.

"Lord almighty," Nelson said and nearly dropped the light. The man had a bandage on his nose and three eyes! The maintenance man forced himself to look again and this time he realized that the third spot was smaller than an eye . . . about the size of a cigarette burn. In fact, that's sort of what it looked like, round and neat and charred around the edges. Except no cigarette could make a hole that deep and there were no butts on the floor next to the creep's head, only a little puddle of something dark and shiny. Nelson shut the light off, stood back up, and grabbed for the bannister. "Don't throw up," he told himself, "won't no one here to clean it up but you, Nelson." He struggled up the staircase and finally found a transit cop in the main waiting room. By then he had managed to regain control over his stomach.

"You better come on down and folla' me," he said solemnly to the fresh-faced rookie. "Looks like someone missed his train."

Forty-one

MARGARET WAS IN HER ROBE AND HER pink gauzy hairnet and had just settled into her favorite armchair when the call came. She lowered that morning's *Times* crossword and scowled. It had been such a busy day she hadn't even had a chance to put in one word yet. It was now nine P.M., a half hour before she usually retired, but there was still plenty of time to finish off the puzzle. Even on her worst days it usually took no more than twenty-five minutes. Her record was eleven and a half minutes but Maleska had given her a gift that weekday. Imagine putting five medieval kings from Ethelred to Cnut in such a small puzzle. She let the phone ring two more times before she decided to answer it.

"Hello."

"Mrs. Binton, it's Sonja. You want to hear what I got?"

Margaret forgot about the puzzle and leaned forward. "Go ahead, I'm listening."

"I got lucky and found Rabin after his second drink and stayed through his fourth. Needless to say, you owe me one. He fancies himself God's great gift to women but I'd say he was more in the category of a manufacturer's rebate."

Margaret frowned into the phone. "Well, I hope he wasn't rude."

"No, he wasn't rude, just arrogant and condescending and drunk."

"And indiscreet?" Margaret said hopefully.

Sonja hesitated. "Well I don't have a name if that's what you mean. I tried but even in his alcoholic fog he clutched to a few principles. But he did say one or two things."

"What?" Margaret asked.

"Well, after a while I brought the conversation around to Rostinkowski and told him that I had clerked for him. 'What a piece of work,' I said. 'Rushes through cases without mercy.' I told him they should change his nickname from Enema Ed to Railroad 'em Rostinkowski. Rabin of course, showing off, disagrees. 'Why just today,' he says, 'I got Rostinkowski down to ten grand on bail for some guy who's been arraigned on a murder one.' 'That's interesting,' I said. 'Your client must have looked like he was a good risk. What was he wearing, an Armani suit?' "

"Very creative," Margaret chuckled.

"So Rabin shook his head and said that the guy had looked like a scuzzball. He didn't even have enough to cover his own bail. 'So who posted it?' I asked innocently. Rabin looks at me. I've now been standing next to him at the bar for close to an hour and we'd covered a lot of distance even before I hit on Rostinkowski. I mean I though his guard was pretty low. He looks at me and says, 'Let's just say, honey, he's got a friend in the right place.' 'So his friend wears Armani suits,' I said. 'Yeah, and hundred-dollar shirts. Very wealthy.' Then he added something about how surprised he was that he got the case."

"Can you remember exactly what he said?" Margaret asked.

Sonja paused before answering. "He said, 'I was surprised that he needed me.' Yeah, I think that's what he said. I got the feeling the guy could afford Cravaith, Swain and Moore."

"Mmmm." Margaret thought that over. "Anything else?"

"That's all. 'It's nice to have friends like that,' I said to keep the conversation going and Rabin says, 'It's nicer to have friends like you.' Then he put his hand a little low on my shoulder, and whispers 'Why the hell are we talking about Rostinkowski when there are more interesting things to talk about? Like my Jacuzzi in Queens."

"Oh my," Margaret said. "I had no idea . . ."

"That's okay, I'm a big girl. It didn't take me too long after that to clear out. I'm afraid that's the best I could do."

"No, no, that's wonderful," Margaret said. "I think I know who we're looking for now. I can't tell you how much I appreciate what you did."

"Save it," Sonja replied. "It's for a good cause."

"I suppose I do owe you one," Margaret said. "How about one perfect little smile from Eric?"

"Payment in full," Sonja said.

"Let's hope he still has one left after the hearing."

Forty-two

"WHAT THE HELL," MORLEY SAID DISGUSTedly. "I send you to do a simple little job and you lose the son of a bitch."

The man standing in front of Morley's desk early the next morning gave him a shrug and shifted uneasily to his other foot. He was in plainclothes and could have passed for a carwash attendant as easily as for a police officer. "Come on, Lieutenant," he answered. "He knew he was going to be followed. The guy made me after ten minutes. I'm supposed to be Houdini or something? I needed a backup."

"Yeah, and a SWAT team I suppose." Morley frowned. "In any case your boy Myrtle wound up yesterday in a stairwell of Penn Station with a copper-jacketed twenty-two caliber bullet in his brain. And from close range no less. Great police work, Simmons. If you had been on the goddamn job we'd at least have a description. Might have even saved the bastard."

If Simmons was surprised, he didn't show it. "Hey, this guy Myrtle was no saint."

"That's supposed to be an excuse for blowing a surveillance? Next time that happens you're out walking a beat in Canarsie." He looked at the younger man angrily. "That's all," he said and went back to reading the homicide report in front of him. Simmons quietly slipped out the door.

"Jesus Christ, now what do I tell Margaret?" Morley said to himself. After a moment's thought he picked up the receiver and dialed her number. The busy signal that came back at him just made him angrier.

Margaret waited while Sid turned off the television in his

tiny apartment. When he got back on the phone Margaret found she didn't have to shout to be heard.

"Can you come over right away? I need some help."

"What, at seven-thirty in the morning? What's the problem?"

"I can't tell you over the phone, Sid. I need you to do a little errand."

"Oh yeah?" He sounded skeptical.

"Okay, I want you to deliver some flowers."

"Getting romantic in your old age?"

"You'll see," she said and hung up before he had a chance to tell her how impossibly early it was. "Now," she said to Eric who was playing on the floor in front of her. "Let's hope this works." She pushed the instrument back on the side table and was about to get up when it rang.

"I will not take no for an answer," she said without hesitation. "I'm expecting you."

"Yeah, to do what?" Morley said, without missing a beat.

"Oh, lieutenant," Margaret sounded flustered. "I thought you were someone else."

"Like who?"

"Like who? What is this?" Margaret regained some of her composure. "I have your permission maybe now and then to see a friend?"

"I just hope it's not a recent acquaintance," Morley said. "Myrtle's dead. He was shot yesterday afternoon."

"Good Lord, this is getting out of hand."

"And it's probably not over. Not until you back off, Margaret. Your fight to keep Eric has already caused two deaths."

"So you condone baby selling?"

"I didn't say that."

"No, but you did say I should back off."

"Yeah, and let me do the work. That doesn't mean Eric's going to become an article of merchandise. The association will find him a good home."

"Maybe," Margaret said. "If he's very lucky. I'm just trying to even the odds, that's all. At the moment I'd say he was on the short end."

"Listen, Margaret," Morley said finally. "I appreciate what you're saying, but I also know we're not dealing here with some underpaid social worker trying to skim off a little on the side. Maybe Regency was like that, but not the person pulling her string. He's killed twice, and he'll go for three if he needs to. I'm telling you, your hearing's in one more day. Start thinking of getting Eric away from all this mess. You can still follow his progress if he's living somewhere else."

"That's like Dallas Green coaching the Yankees from Hackensack."

"Margaret, enough with the jokes. I'm serious. So serious in fact, I'm grounding you for the next twenty-four hours. You need something, you let me know and I'll arrange for it."

Margaret looked down at the floor, where her little foster son was still playing, and took a deep breath.

"You think it's dangerous for us to go out?"

"I do. He's tried to have you killed once already."

"Okay, Sam," she said into the phone after another moment. "I promise I won't go out until after the hearing. I'll double-lock my door if it makes you feel any better. But I can't guarantee what will happen tomorrow when they ask me to give up Eric." She took a deep breath. "What'd Wright have to say when you saw him?"

"Four words—'Speak to my lawyer.' All the attention is driving him crazy."

"But not so crazy to call off the hearing."

"He claims Regency's death was drug related. It was in Ryker's story this morning. Ryker called me up for confirmation yesterday so I proposed a little trade. I told him I was curious where he got his information from."

"Not from me if that's what you were thinking."

"It was a possibility. But he said it was an anonymous phone call came in out of the blue. He wasn't going to print it unless I confirmed it."

"And?"

"I'm not in the habit of lying to the press."

"Damn," Margaret said. "No doubt the person who called was the person who planted the drugs . . . to take the heat off the agency. That's not good for Eric in tomorrow's hearing." Margaret hesitated. "You going to be there?"

"I was thinking of it. In fact, to be on the safe side, I was thinking of bringing you."

"Fine," Margaret said. "Why don't you come when my friend Berdie arrives, around nine. She's going to help with Eric."

"See you then."

"Oh, and Sam, don't worry, I'll be careful." She hung the phone up and stayed motionless for a few minutes, thinking. Then she sank down to the floor next to Eric and began helping him with his blocks.

When the doorbell rang a half hour later, Margaret and Eric had something approaching Mad Ludwig's castle rising from the floor. Margaret got up to open the door as the little boy put the finishing touches to the central tower. Sid just made it over the doorstep when he heard a loud crash.

"What was that?" he asked nervously.

"I like to think of it as deconstruction," Margaret said. "Come in."

Sid picked his way into the living room and sat down heavily on the sofa. "I rushed right over. What's this about a flower delivery?"

Margaret reached into a nearby drawer and pulled out a pencil and piece of paper. She scribbled down something quickly and handed it back to him.

"There's the address and below that is what I want you to get. I don't think you need anything fancy, I can't afford more than say, five or six dollars. But they must be carnations."

Sid peered closely at the little note. "And that's all?" he asked.

She gave him a few more instructions about getting the receipt. "And when you finish, come straight back here."

"What's the deal?" Sid asked, confused. "A bunch of flowers is so important I gotta miss my 'Good Morning America'?"

"Vital," she said. "It's going to catch us a murderer. Now, I want that delivered in person. If you can't, just come back and we'll try later in the afternoon."

"Do I have time for a coffee?" Sid asked wistfully, looking in the direction of Margaret's kitchen.

"A potful when you get back," she said. "Now hurry."

* * *

After she had closed the door behind Sid, Margaret went back to the phone. Eric was still sitting next to the pile of blocks but now he was pretending to be a bomber pilot. The sound of wood crashing into wood punctured Margaret's brain.

"Hello?" Peter Ryker's sleepy voice came from the other end of the line.

"Peter, it's Margaret. I'm sorry but I had to call you at home. I gather you're still working on the YBA story?"

"Are you kidding? With the Regency death I can't keep my editor off my back. Now with the drug angle it's getting crazy."

"Forget the drug angle, I have another piece of information for you, but I want to make a deal—a little give and take."

"What's that noise in the background?"

"Just Eric playing."

"Give and take . . . what does that mean?" Ryker asked.

"I give you some information that hasn't leaked to the press yet, and take back your promise to do something for me."

Ryker blew his nose. "Margaret, how come all of a sudden you're turning formal on me? I don't like deals. Information I can always use, but promises in this business are rare."

"How about a favor then?"

"Maybe. Like what?"

"Tomorrow's Eric's hearing. I want you to cover it. I mean with a photographer and all. I realize Eric is not really in the center of your story, but having the press there, even if they aren't allowed in the room, will be a big help."

Ryker hesitated for only a moment. "I suppose I can arrange that."

"Good, I have a feeling it will be worth your while. Now, you got a pencil, take this down. William Myrtle, shot yesterday at Penn Station, was the guy that did all the withdrawals for Regency's boss up at Lucky's. He was also the man that tried to give me a diving lesson."

"How's that?"

"Never mind. I'll tell you when I see you tomorrow. Ten o'clock at the YBA offices."

"I'll be there but hold on—"

"Sorry, Peter, I have to run. Eric is about to do an experiment to see if bricks bounce when dropped from six stories.

Tomorrow—bye.'' She hung up quickly and made it over to the window before Eric had a chance to push a block through the protective bars.

''Time for breakfast,'' she said.

Forty-three

SID HAND-PICKED THE DOZEN CARNA-tions at an all-night Korean delicatessen on Amsterdam to make sure they were absolutely fresh. Margaret had said the colors didn't matter, so he improvised, mixing reds in with hot pinks and some electric green-flecked whites that made his bouquet look like it belonged in a fauvist still life. The grocer surveyed his handiwork with some reservations, but wrapped it anyway after Sid slipped a little note inside. Two minutes after getting his change Sid was on a number 104 bus heading down Broadway to Seventy-fourth Street. From there it was just a short walk to West End Avenue.

Apart from maybe the mailman and the United Parcel representative, most delivery people in New York are no longer in uniform. Gone are the more formal days when even diaper deliveries were made by immaculately uniformed men with little peaked caps and friendly manners. Nowadays, when you opened the door in Manhattan, chances were you'd be receiving a parcel from someone dressed in sneakers and a sweatshirt who doubled as a waiter, or from some messenger with a black leather jacket and wraparound shades who looked like he just stepped off the set of *Road Warrior*. A pleasant-looking older gentleman with an obvious bouquet of flowers presented no problem to the doorman of the luxury apartment building, even if it was only eight o'clock in the morning. Sid gave the name and was nodded on through to the self-service elevator and told to go up to 12F.

The hallway on the twelfth floor was a long affair with several doors leading off it. The doorman had apparently called ahead because as Sid emerged from the elevator, one of the doors opened and a man leaned against the jamb. Sid followed the letters in his direction—C, D, E . . .

"This is F," the man said. "What is it?"

He was dressed in a business suit and looked as if he had just been eating breakfast. He held a napkin in his hand and Sid could just get the smell of bacon wafting out of his door.

"Flowers for Mr . . . ," Sid looked up at the ticket he had taped to the top of the bouquet and read off a name.

"Yeah, that's me. So early?"

"You call this early?" Sid said. "You're my third delivery. You'd be surprised how many arguments happen between dinner and breakfast."

"Who are they from?" the man asked but Sid just raised an eyebrow. "I just deliver them, Mac, I don't sell them." He handed the bouquet over and took a pen and piece of paper out of his shirt pocket. "Do me a favor though, will you. Take a look at them. My boss is getting on my case after he got a call I crushed a delivery last week. Guy probably sat on them after I left. I think these are the carnations." Sid took out a little knife and made a slit at the top of the wrapping. "Yeah, dozen mixed carnations. Just sign this and then write that the carnations arrived in good shape, will ya? Son of a bitch wouldn't trust his own mother with a dead petunia." Sid held out the pen and piece of paper. The man looked at the paper, then back up at the wrapped flowers and frowned.

"You don't know who they're from?" he said, more to himself.

"I think there's a card inside."

"So where are you from—the flower shop?"

Sid hesitated for a split second, then said the first thing that popped into his head.

"Acme Florist over on Columbus."

The man enlarged the slit until the carnations popped out of the enclosed wrappings. As the man continued looking for the card, Sid pushed the pen on him.

"Sorry to rush you, Mac, but I got a lot more deliveries to do. They look okay to you?"

The man stopped rummaging and looked up at the flowers.

"Yeah, yeah. What do you want?"

"Just your name and that the carnations were okay."

The man impatiently balanced the bouquet in the crook of his arm, leaned the paper against the wall and signed under a one line note. He hesitated, reached into his pocket, and removed fifty cents in change. He handed the note and the pen and the two quarters back to Sid.

"Here."

Sid pocketed the change then turned and walked toward the elevator. By the time the doors opened, the man had found the note. Sid saw him staring at the small piece of paper and then the automatic doors closed tight. Sid had kept the message simple. "From a secret admirer," it said and was designed to allow him to leave without being stopped by the doorman or being followed. After all, Margaret had reasoned, in everyone's heart there's always room for a secret admirer, even in the heart of a murderer.

But Sid had made a serious mistake in giving the name of the purported florist shop. There were a lot of Acmes in the telephone book, but between Acme Exterminating and Acme Frocks there was no listing for Acme Florists. This curious omission was spotted three minutes after Sid rounded the corner on Broadway by the man looking suspiciously from his vase of fresh carnations to his telephone book. He didn't move for several minutes, as he doodled something with his pen on a piece of paper. Something he wrote caught his attention and he leaned closer.

"Son of a bitch!" he said and stabbed his pen down into one of the words. "How did she find out?"

Forty-four

THE REST OF THE DAY PASSED BY AT A LAbored pace for Margaret. Sid returned and stayed for two cups of coffee, then made it down to the newsstand for the early edition of the *Telegraph*. He'd be gone for the rest of the day, Margaret thought, or at least until the last race at OTB. Eric tired of the blocks twenty minutes after breakfast and it was downhill from there. If only she hadn't given Morley her word she wouldn't go out. Margaret knew the park would be full of children playing in the sun. It was where Eric should have been instead of cooped up inside a stuffy one-bedroom apartment. But a promise was a promise, so she opened all the windows to let in more fresh air, even the one by the fire escape, and spent the afternoon reading and playing with the little boy.

At two o'clock, Berdie came by for a chat. Eric was taking a nap with his pink panther and the two older women spent a pleasant hour talking. If Margaret was all keyed up for the next day's meeting she didn't show it to Berdie, who left shortly after three with instructions to come back the following morning at nine. Morley called back a half hour later to check that Margaret was keeping her word and to reconfirm that he was planning to escort her in the morning to the hearing. Alice called from the center, wondering why she hadn't stopped by with Eric, and the handyman came up to reset the drain washer on the bathroom faucet finally. For the rest of the afternoon it was either story-time, with Aesop's fables, Maurice Sendak, and Dr. Seuss, or playing demolition derby on the rug with Eric's Matchbox cars.

By dinner Margaret was exhausted and longing for bed. In her mind, everything was ready for the hearing. She had her arguments rehearsed, her evidence in hand, and her troops marshalled. All she needed was a little luck.

Eric had started climbing out of his crib two weeks earlier, so Margaret was now putting him to sleep in Oscar's old twin bed. Positioned right up against her bed, it had long been used as an extended night table for books in the process of being read, ashtrays, finished crossword puzzles, even at one point her collection of handbags. Margaret felt good about it being resurrected into the bed it was. The crib was pushed against the open side to keep Eric from falling out and the life-sized pink panther that Ryker had given him was tucked under his blanket on the near side as a buffer. Eric was not the best sleeper and on several occasions Margaret had woken up and been surprised to see him talking to one of his stuffed animals on the bed. His favorite, though, was the pink panther; a few times their conversations actually roused her from deep sleep. She often wondered what Eric was talking about in his baby-talk patter in the small hours of the night but the panther never betrayed a secret. He bore it all in silence, including the eye-poking, fur-pulling and nose-tweaking. Margaret figured that the panther was good for an additional hour of sleep per night.

Once again before putting him to bed she checked that all the doors were closed, the room free of hazards from tiny prying fingers, and the window slightly open for fresh air. A locked diamond window gate ensured that Eric couldn't crawl out to the fire escape on the other side. She sang him a bedtime song, and watched with relief as his eyes slowly closed and he slipped off to sleep. She watched him for a few more minutes in silence as he curled up under the thin blanket with one arm around his panther's neck, looking, for all the world, so tiny and vulnerable. She realized that seventy-two years of life finally came to this. It didn't matter so much what you once did, where you've been, who your friends were. What was more important was how you responded to the little cries for help, the calls of loneliness, of fear, and of trust. After a moment she sighed and got up. No crossword tonight, not even a few minutes of television. She wanted to be fresh in the morning to meet Mr. Wright and all the lawyers and other people trying to take Eric away.

She checked the double lock on the front door, got into her flannel nightgown, put her hairnet on, and crawled into the bed next to Eric and pink panther. She switched the light off and closed her eyes.

But there was no one to sing her a lullaby, and after forty-five minutes of staring at the shadows on the ceiling, she groaned and grudgingly got back out of bed. Typical, she thought, insomnia before an important morning, like bread landing on the buttered side when it fell. Why was life like that? She made her way out to the living room, closed the door behind her, and found the morning's crossword puzzle. Half an hour at most, she figured. She propped herself up in her comfortable arm chair, and started filling in the empty blanks.

Sleep finally hit her with the force of a Peruvian mudslide once her mind was off her next day's visit. She was on thirty-four across—swamp denizen—when her pencil slipped between her fingers and her chin sank slowly to her chest. Her breathing became heavier, but not so loud as to be heard in the other room.

It was another noise that woke Eric from his sleep several hours later, a scraping and metallic sound that came from the direction of the window. He sat up in bed and in his little seventeen-month-old mind must have thought he was still dreaming. There, framed behind the diamond grid of the window gate, was a man's face . . . floating. But if it was a dream it was not a friendly dream and the little boy huddled closer to the crib on his right, comforted by the familiar slats. He stayed that way and watched while the floating face, illuminated only by a tiny night light near the radiator, moved inside the frame of the window.

The man cursed softly to himself. It was hard to see inside with the dim light at floor level. The beds were in shadow and all he could make out was the tiny form of the boy's legs next to the crib, and a hump in the middle of the two beds that was probably the old lady. Dim, very dim, but it was the only other form in the bed and everything else was quiet. God, it had to be her. One A.M. she's got to be in bed, he thought.

Slowly he eased himself down until his eye was just at the

level of the open window, then carefully poked the barrel of the longnose twenty-two-caliber pistol, made longer with its three-inch silencer, through the opening. With just a little squirming causing a minimum of sound, he brought the rear sight in line with the large sleeping form, held it for the space of a deep breath, then pulled the trigger four times. Four popping noises filled the room, not louder than the opening of four cans of soda, and the blanket three feet away from Eric danced backwards. The boy clutched the crib but made no sounds. His eyes were taking it all in but he wasn't willing to say anything for fear the floating face would look directly at him and the blanket would move again, like a snake was underneath. He watched, and slowly the face drifted left, then right, then mysteriously floated away. The metallic noise came back again, then finally everything was silent. Eric eased back down into the bed and turned his head away. What he couldn't see couldn't hurt him. He threw an arm over pink panther again and nuzzled a smaller plush teddy bear by his pillow. In five minutes he was asleep again.

At five A.M. Margaret woke up in the armchair and sleepily stumbled back to bed. She managed to sleep through her alarm and was finally woken by another noise. Eric was wailing right next to her, crying his little lungs out, and Margaret propped herself up on one elbow, rubbed her nose, then opened her eyes to see what was the matter. Eric was sitting in the middle of the bed holding on to pink panther . . . or rather to the remains of pink panther. His sleek head was blown out from front to back and the stuffing around his upper chest was hanging out in one big mushroom clump. Two other holes penetrated the poor animal's cotton fur around his abdomen with similar consequences to his back. The bed was littered with an explosion of stuffing. At first Margaret didn't understand—why had he destroyed his favorite toy? It didn't make sense. Then her eye caught sight of something that made it all clear, a slim, metallic object that was lying right on top of the pillow by her elbow. It had a copper-colored jacket, and from close range looked as deadly as any larger-caliber bullet. Her stifled cry only managed to frighten Eric into her arms, where the two of them stayed until Margaret recovered.

"Oh, Eric," she finally managed, "I'm sorry."

"Bad man," he said, and pointed towards the window.

"Did you see?" Margaret asked.

"Bad man," Eric repeated and pushed the panther away from him. "Make panther boo-boo."

She asked her question again and Eric looked up into her eyes with such pain that she held him closer and said "never mind." But she knew he had seen and oh my God how he must have been frightened. And she hadn't even been in the room to comfort him. But then she realized with a chill that if she had, the stuffing on the bed would be her own instead of the cotton doll's. Thank God for insomnia, she thought, and went to close and cover the window.

Forty-five

IF ANY WERE SURPRISED WHEN MARGARET entered the hearing room at ten o'clock that morning, they were keeping it to themselves. Seven faces turned toward her with varying expressions but no one's jaw dropped. Morley identified himself to the referee assigned by the state Department of Social Services, then took a seat over in a corner. Already in the room were a stenographer; Mr. Wright with the lawyer for the agency; Jason Sawyer; Eric's legal guardian, Sonja Miller; and both Mr. and Mrs. Victor Lazarre. The Lazarres' presence in the room was something of a shock to Margaret until she realized the probable altered YBA strategy. They would go for another foster placement as Wright had said, but the new foster parents would be the Lazarres. It was a nice bureaucratic nuance that protected the agency and kept the Lazarres at the head of the list. Why hadn't Margaret seen it coming?

The nine people did a good job of filling up the small room. They gathered around the scratched YBA conference table, which doubled as a skittles play surface when the older kids were allowed in for recreation. The walls had travel posters Scotch-taped to the plaster board, a cheap but insensitive decorating solution to the problems of a slow cash flow. If ever one of their charges "let the sun and transparent waters of Jamaica caress them," it would be on an August afternoon by a Queens fire hydrant. She looked around the room and saw to her dismay that no one else was sporting the animated and friendly smiles of Mickey and Minnie Mouse in their Disney World poster. In fact, everyone else looked quite annoyed.

"Mrs. Binton," Mr. Wright began, "was it your idea to call in the press?"

She cleared her throat. "In view of what's happened, I thought it might be newsworthy."

"What has happened has nothing to do with what will go on in this room." He turned to the referee, one Anthony Landine, a middle-aged, unfashionable-looking gentleman who bore a close resemblance to George Wilson on the old "Dennis the Menace" reruns. "Two mini-cam crews and a slew of reporters," he continued, searching for an ally. "You saw what a hard time I had just keeping them out of the room."

"I did," Landine said, "and I want to say at the outset that I find their presence highly irregular. This hearing is merely a fact-finding procedure. I will conduct it like every other one. This issue here is Eric Williams' placement and ultimate future. The department has certain guidelines and procedures, which I intend to follow." He stopped for a breath. "First of all I will hear arguments for his removal from Mr. Wright of the agency, take a statement from his legal guardian, Ms. Miller, then his foster mother will have an opportunity to offer her comments. I want to assure everyone that I have read the case history already, including all correspondence."

Margaret raised her eyes in disbelief toward Morley, who merely shook his head slowly from side to side. This was insane. Landine was playing this as though three days of Ryker's stories hadn't appeared in the papers and a criminal investigation wasn't next on the agenda downtown. Bureaucrats, she thought angrily to herself and reached into her handbag for her cigarettes.

"I'm sorry, Mrs. Binton," Jason Sawyer said. "There's no smoking in this room."

She glowered at him, then at the rest of them, but left her pack where it was.

"Before we begin," Sawyer continued. "We'd like to know where Eric Williams is now."

"He is in the next room with my friend, Mrs. Mangione," Margaret said. "I suspect he is being well looked after, considering that when I left him he was surrounded by two television crews. Also my friend Peter Ryker is with him."

"Accessible," Sawyer added, turning to Landine with a tiny smile. The referee didn't comment.

"If you think you can take Eric today," Margaret said quickly, "you are mistaken. The regulations specifically say that the referee must hand down a written decision within thirty days."

"I'd like to point out that *within* is not the same as *after*," Jason Sawyer said. "And we have a typist on call." He looked at her with such a smug expression that Margaret felt her hand close into a fist. This was starting to sound like a kangaroo court.

"So, if you want to start, Mr. Wright," Landine said, "go ahead."

Wright cleared his throat, removed some papers from a beat-up briefcase by his chair, and slapped them on the table.

"From the very first," he began, "Mrs. Binton has been a problem." He went on to read the reports detailing what a nuisance she had been, specifically obstructing the medical scheduling at the same time bringing in her foster child with a chronic cold.

"Your building was overheated," Margaret grumbled, "and the scheduling was not a problem when I was conferred with."

"You'll get your turn," Landine interjected.

"She was counseled from the very first that this was a temporary placement," Wright continued. "It is unfortunate and tragic that Mrs. Regency cannot be here today, but were she able I am sure she would confirm this fact; Mrs. Binton, from the very first, acted unprofessionally as a foster parent—she was totally unable to separate her personal emotions from her role. Keeping Eric Williams with her now will only make matters that much harder later."

"Mrs. Regency is, as you say, 'unfortunately unable to be with us today' because she was murdered," Morley said sarcastically from the corner.

"Please, Lieutenant Morley," Landine said. "You're not part of this."

"Not yet," Morley said and leaned back in his chair.

"Continue," Mr. Landine said to Wright.

"Eric needs a permanent home, there's no question about that. But given the circumstances that this case has raised some interest in the press—because, I might add, of the efforts of the current foster mother—this agency feels that the child should, for the time being, be placed in another foster situation.'' He took a breath. ''Now this agency has found and has proposed a family . . .'' he nodded in the direction of the Lazarres at the end of the table, ''who we feel would provide a loving, healthy environment for little Eric, temporarily, of course, until some of the questions raised in the press about the adoption selection process have been dealt with. I would like to leave that discussion up to our attorney, Mr. Sawyer.''

Sawyer, sitting in the next chair, straightened up noticeably.

''The agency is under a spotlight at this moment,'' he said. ''But I want to assure you that nothing improper has happened or will happen with any of our placements. It is indeed unfortunate that Mrs. Helen Regency, who was mentioned in some of the stories, is not able to defend herself. When it came to running the Association's adoption processes, she was a loyal, hard-working professional, and I for one do not believe the slanderous things that have been said about her in that regard. Where she erred tragically was in getting involved with drugs, which had nothing to do with her duties for this organization. There is, apparently, evidence of that, as reported in the press. In the meantime, I can guarantee you that to my knowledge, there have been absolutely no payments by anyone in the case of Eric Williams.''

Margaret couldn't control herself. ''I don't believe what I'm hearing,'' she said. ''This little farce of a hearing goes on as though the outside world doesn't exist. There have been payments in the past . . . there are witnesses.''

Landine interrupted. ''This is not a criminal proceeding, Mrs. Binton, the issue is Eric Williams.''

''And the bucks didn't stop at Regency . . .''

Landine raised his voice. ''You will have your turn, Mrs. Binton.'' He looked to his left. ''Right now, Ms. Miller, as Eric's legal guardian you have an obligation to speak in his behalf.''

The room quieted while Sonja leaned forward. She looked around the table, gave a little encouraging smile to Margaret, and shook her head.

''I'd like to try and be clear on this. I do think that Eric should be placed in a permanent home with two parents and as soon as possible. However, I am not convinced that the agency has found the right solution in going for another temporary situation or that given the current clouded atmosphere, the move should be made right now. Given the choices facing this hearing, I'd vote for nonremoval." She looked over and caught Margaret's smile.

"Thank you," Landine said.

"Can I say something?" Victor Lazarre asked.

"No, you're just here as a guest of the Youth Benevolent Association," Landine shot back. "You have no right to say anything. Now," he looked around the room and his gaze finally came to rest on Margaret. "It's your turn."

"Finally," she said, and stood up. She pushed her chair back and stepped into the space between the wall and the chairs.

"Now," she began. "I want you all, especially Mr. Landine, to be aware that we are not only talking about the placement of a little child here, we are talking about a baby-selling scheme and two murders. No matter what Mr. Sawyer or Mr. Wright say, this agency was a part of it. It's true there has yet to be a trial and conviction, but what has transpired must not be overlooked as though it was pure fiction. As I said, there is a witness to at least one payoff. I know because I interviewed her myself."

"Two murders?" Sawyer said. "Who else?"

"William Myrtle," Morley supplied. "The guy who drowned Regency. He also tried to do the same to Mrs. Binton. Whoever killed him did the state a favor."

"But why?" Sawyer persisted.

"To keep him from talking." Margaret continued. "He knew exactly how the payoffs were worked through Regency and who was on the receiving end. Ryker, Morley, and I also knew the mechanics, but we didn't know who was pulling Regency's and Myrtle's strings. Then yesterday I got the proof I needed."

"You didn't tell me that this morning," Morley said in surprise. This hearing was taking on a new direction.

"I also didn't tell you that he must have found out I knew and tried to kill me again last night. Only this time he had to do it himself." She smiled at him. "As you can see, once again luck was a lady—or in my case, a five-foot stuffed animal. Mrs. Mangione brought it along when she brought Eric so I could show everyone." She turned towards Landine. "I'd also like to bring Eric in for a moment."

Landine looked at her closely, then nodded. "I'd like to see the boy, too, but if I ask you to remove him, he goes, no questions."

Margaret moved the few feet to the door, opened it quickly, and passed through. Within a half minute she came back, leading Eric by the hand and carrying a bulky object in a large plastic garbage bag. Slowly she leaned over and shook the bag onto the table. The pink panther with its cotton viscera slid out in front of everyone.

"This was supposed to have been me," she said and reached into a pocket. "And this is what did the damage." She placed the bullet in front of Morley. "I suspect that it will be a perfect match with the bullet that killed Myrtle. Unfortunately Eric saw everything." She leaned down and lifted the little boy up onto the table. "While there's no way we can help him erase his painful memory of it, I was hoping he could help us identify who stuck that gun through the open window and brazenly pulled the trigger four times. With your permission . . ." she said and spun Eric slowly until he was facing the people around the table.

"Eric," she said softly, "Show Margaret who gave pink panther his boo-boo."

Eric looked back up at Margaret and frowned.

"Go ahead," she coached. "He won't hurt you."

"You gotta be kidding," Victor Lazarre said. "A *baby*?"

Eric crawled onto the center of the table, right next to the destroyed panther, and flipped back up to a sitting position. He looked at the first person across from him, then carefully let his eyes travel around the table. First there was Landine, then the stenographer, then Sonja. Suddenly he pointed.

"Bad man," he cried. "Make panther boo-boo. Bad man."

Everyone in the room followed his arm, everyone except the person he was pointing at.

"This is ridiculous," Jason Sawyer said. "He can hardly talk."

"But he can point," Morley said leaning forward. Eric's finger was aiming right for Sawyer's heart.

"That's really going to stand up in court," the lawyer said. "Don't make me laugh."

Margaret walked around the table a few steps until she was standing behind Landine. Eric crawled over and sat right in front of him.

"So many things led me to you, Mr. Sawyer, not just that Eric saw you trying to shoot me. Right away I suspected when I heard that the killer was using the pseudonym of Henry D. Bracton." She turned to the others around the table. "I can't imagine why he was so obvious. Bracton is really a household name, a famous thirteenth-century lawyer who wrote a treatise on the laws and customs of England—the bible, I might add, in the history of English law."

"In what households?" Morley asked.

"Well, certainly in any household that is serious about crosswords." She took a few steps further and wound up behind the stenographer. "That's Bracton," she corrected. "No 'k.' You'll see why later. Now, that pointed to a scholar or lawyer, of course, but it was only a direction. There were two other things that caught my attention. After Regency was murdered, Lieutenant Morley found a considerable quantity of drugs in her desk at the association that, for whatever it's worth, were not there when I had an unauthorized look a few days earlier. But what's more interesting is that as the lawyer for a private organization linked to a nasty murder, Sawyer should have delayed Morley's investigation of Regency's work space—at the very least require he have the correct search warrants. But instead he didn't say a peep and all but pointed him in the right direction." She turned to Morley. "Did you in fact have a warrant when you went in?"

Morley shook his head.

"And there wasn't an objection because Sawyer wanted the drugs found right where he planted them, to miscue the investigation. Very unprofessional for a lawyer whose job it is to look after the interests of his employer." Margaret shook her head.

"But what put the icing on the cake for me was a little information I got from Sonja. She told me that Mr. Rabin, the lawyer who handled Myrtle's bail hearing, confided that the man who put up the money was wealthy. Rabin also said that 'he was surprised that he needed him.' Sonja misconstrued that comment to mean that Myrtle's benefactor could have hired the most expensive lawyers in town. But Rabin was surprised quite simply because his client was a lawyer himself and could have easily handled a simple bail hearing.

"You can't be serious," Sawyer said. "First you get a toddler to accuse me, then you try to implicate me further because I don't obstruct an officer from carrying out an investigation and finally simply because I'm a lawyer. It's laughable."

"I didn't say this was the proof," Margaret said, "These things just pointed the way. The proof came in the form of a receipt for an innocent little delivery of carnations. I was able to match up the letters on the receipt with a withdrawal slip from Lucky's pawn shop signed by the mysterious Henry D. Bracton."

"How'd you get that?" Morley asked angrily.

"Oh, when you showed them to me and they slipped to the floor it wasn't quite so accidental. Sorry, Sam, you had so many; I only needed one." She shrugged. "The man I sent the flowers to wrote in an unguarded moment, "The carnations arrived okay," and signed his real name, Jason Sawyer. You'll notice the only letters from Henry Bracton not included in this note is the 'B'. A handwriting expert should have no trouble confirming the similarities." She turned to Jason Sawyer. "Even to my untrained eye the similarities are obvious." She reached into her pocket and withdrew a piece of paper. "You don't deny you wrote this yesterday, because if you do, I have a witness that will challenge that."

"This is absurd," Sawyer said. "The issue here is placing a child for adoption, not listening to the fantasies of an old woman."

"No," Mr. Landine said, leaning away from Eric, who was trying to grab his tie. "The issue is trust, and I think I've heard enough unanswered questions here to give pause to the most indifferent referee. I'm not sure there shouldn't be criminal charges brought just on the basis of this information, but that's not my job." He turned to Margaret.

"You'll get my report in a week, but it's going to say that you can keep Eric until things get straightened out here. I hope that when it finally comes time to place Eric permanently the agency will be smart enough to review and act on your suggestions. As for you, Wright, I'd start looking around for another job. I'm assuming you knew nothing of what went on, but, for God's sake, you were supposed to." He stood up. "This hearing is over. As far as I'm concerned you can let in the press."

"Just a minute—" Mr. Wright began, but was soon silenced by the rush of the opening door and the flurry of reporters. Margaret had responded promptly to Landine's suggestion.

"What's going on?" Ryker was the first to ask. "What's the story here? Where's Eric going?"

Morley stood up and walked next to Sawyer. "Eric stays," he said. "This one goes. I'm taking him in for murder, attempted murder, conspiracy to murder, and some lesser charges involving the illegal trafficking of children." He started moving him out.

Ryker's pen was moving fast but he could hardly keep up. After he got it all down he looked up at Margaret.

"Motive?" he said.

"Money surely. Easy money because it was just so accessible. The YBA children, all the other agencies he works for, a private referral now and then—all channeled through Regency. With any luck, if Lazarre is offered immunity, he might testify about his own payment to get Eric. I think Morley can get all the pieces together."

Ryker grinned. "It may not be a Pulitzer," he said, "but it might get me a raise."

"Good, you'll need it," she answered. "Eric likes movies and nice clothes and, when he's old enough, a trip to Disney World."

"How's that?" Ryker asked.

"Just in case you and Janet were still thinking of adopting." She winked. "I think I know a little someone who's available."

About the Author

RICHARD BARTH is a goldsmith and an instructor at the Fashion Institute of Technology. He lives in Manhattan with his wife and two children. THE RAG BAG CLAN was the first book in the Margaret Binton mystery series.